Sarah Tytler

**Sapphira**

Vol. II

Sarah Tytler

**Sapphira**
*Vol. II*

ISBN/EAN: 9783337048013

Printed in Europe, USA, Canada, Australia, Japan

Cover: Foto ©Andreas Hilbeck / pixelio.de

More available books at **www.hansebooks.com**

# SAPPHIRA.

## A Novel.

BY

SARAH TYTLER,

AUTHOR OF

"CITOYENNE JACQUELINE," "LOGIE TOWN," &c., &c.

IN TWO VOLUMES.

VOL. II.

WARD & DOWNEY,

12, YORK STREET, COVENT GARDEN, LONDON.

1890.

# CONTENTS.

# SAPPHIRA.

*" His wife also being privy to it."*

# SAPPHIRA.

## CHAPTER I.

### HIDING THEIR HEADS.

As soon as Georgie got it into her practical little head that it was an astonishing fact, and no fancy, a solemn reality and no bad joke, that the whole family were to start that night for the Continent, she wasted no more precious time on the why and the wherefore. Inquiries and speculations might intrude themselves urgently on her preoccupied mind, but they could wait greater leisure for their solution. What she and everybody else had to do at the present moment was to get ready to go, if they must go on the expedition. It was strange and unaccountable that they must, but the strangeness and unaccountability must also wait for an explanation. So must the undreamt-of wrong-doing and retribution—of which, somehow, Mrs. Baldwin knew as well as Pat, the mere distant, vague conception of which burned, nevertheless, with a painful burning crimson on Georgie's cheeks as she ran up and down stairs, lugging out trunks, emptying drawers, folding up dresses. Her ungrudging, unmurmuring activity was a reproach to Agnes. She was no longer thinking of resisting or of withdrawing from the others and taking no part in their flight. As Pat had said, when his mother consented, Agnes must yield. And what she minded was not the going, the breaking up in an instant of her whole previous life, with its cherished associations and one engrossing occupation. It was the fatal admission, that by some disastrous departure from the straight path of ordinary humanity, her mother was in danger and had to flee. There had been at the very least some cowardly failure, and still more cowardly evasion, where truth and righteousness come into play. There had been some great destructive flaw in what Agnes had fondly judged flawless, which rendered such an unusual step called for, that the household should gather up their goods and decamp, like evil-doers and outcasts. She had been warned, it is true ; but the very warning still lingered in her mind as a wild fancy, a glaring insult, the distorted imagery of a horrible dream, any glimmering confirmation of which in her mother's habits and in the faint recollection of childhood, she had been fighting against gloomily. Agnes rose up languidly and tried to get her papers and a few of her books and clothes in order, though with regard to the former, she had the strongest conviction that she would never write again.

How could she when the whole universe was crumbling about her head, when the household goddess she had enthroned and ardently worshipped was dethroned, covered with some mysterious disgrace, and as it were sitting abjectly in the dust?

For the first time in her life, Agnes occupied herself entirely with herself and her own concerns. She did not offer to assist anybody; she left her mother to Georgie. Mrs. Baldwin marked the change, and looked with a curious timidity and wistfulness at Agnes, who did not meet her mother's eyes or return her look. Then the mother made as if she would do her own packing, at which Georgie cried out loudly as at the greatest absurdity which had been proposed for many a day. She took Mrs. Baldwin's knitting out of her hands and was about to put it up with other effects which could not be done without, but the elder woman interposed : " Don't trouble,

Georgie; I believe I shall not want it ever again," she said with a long sigh. "I think I have come to hate it. I believe I should shudder at the sight of it if it were brought out in new surroundings."

Again Georgie collapsed for a second and stood looking incredulously at her mother, till she took herself to task with the rousing, usurping reminder that they were all going abroad this very night and that there was, of course, an immense deal to do, and hardly anybody save herself to do it. For Agnes, who had hitherto been a pillar of strength in difficulties, was somehow stricken down and walking about as if in a bad dream. Mother could not be suffered to exert herself with so much fatigue before her. Pat, who had suddenly superseded Agnes as head of the house, had enough to do in other respects, while he looked dead in earnest and fully determined on this unheard-of proceeding. He paid the aggrieved Selina wages and board for a month in advance. He did not stop to hear her protest that in all her families with whom she had lived she had never heard of such a doing as this here. But what was to be expected from a missus as sat, month in, month out, like a pillar of salt or Lot's wife, and only bestirred herself to receive a crazy old serving-man. Or what was to be expected from a miss as was always a-scribbling, scribbling, when she was not running all over London. "Books," Miss Georgie said, very like. Then was it books that gave her another name? Selina could take her Bible oath that when the postman brought a letter, not directed as it ought to have been to "Miss Baldwin," but to a "Miss Judith Westmoreland," or some such play-acting title, and asked, civil enough, if a lady as answered to the name lived there, just when she, Selina, was in the act of saying "no" positively—for what had they or other respectable females to do with any " Miss Judith Westmoreland ? "—out darted Miss Baldwin. Though her nose was mostly in her ink bottle, she had heard every word that was said. " Stop, Selina ; stop, postman," she says ; " that letter is for me," as cock-sure and as bold as brass. No good comes of ways unlike other people's, and least of all of made names and moonlight flittings. Selina's last family were a queer lot and she was well quit of them. By the time she came to this conclusion, Selina devoted the moments that were left to changing her dress, making a minute inventory of her wardrobe and packing her box. She disdained to lend a helping hand to such objectionable employers.

" Little Baldwin " in his new capacity did wonders, besides stuffing his portmanteaus. He looked up the keys and locked the outer premises. He wrote addresses. He communicated his ap-

proaching departure to the dispensary and
to the house agent—referring the latter to
Sam Scrope. He summoned a caretaker
who had once before been in the house
for a week ; ah ! that was in such different
circumstances, when Agnes had insisted on
taking the family for a flying visit to the
seaside, in order that Georgie might the
sooner recover from an attack of influenza.
Then, not to say the patient, everybody,
including even Mrs. Baldwin, had been
sensible of a mild elation.

There was no elation in anybody's
spirits to-day when Pat, as the last occu-
pant, drew down the sitting-room window
blinds after he had sent the caretaker to
fetch a cab.

It was a slight consolation to Georgie,
in the middle of her share in the family
trouble, to be conscious how much depended on her, and that the precipitate
act which Pat had inaugurated, and her
mother authorized, could not have been

carried through, even at the last moment, but for her, Georgie's, faithful efforts to promote the inevitable. For the Baldwins, who had, as a rule, been notably domestic and methodical in their performances, did, to the mystification of their neighbours, their dependants, nay, to some of themselves, start in a body for the Continent that same night. Nobody came to help and see them away, and what was more wonderful, perhaps, nobody sought to interfere with them or stay them; though no doubt Pat and Sam Scrope together could have explained the supineness of the agent. The house bills had been paid weekly, with admirable punctuality, by Georgie. No tradesman felt warranted, as yet, in doubting the family credit, though the sudden swift exodus was both suspicious and alarming.

There is always something which savours of mystery and adventure in a night train and a night voyage, which fitted in with the peculiar circumstances of the Baldwins, and caused all the young people to fall under the spell and be partly carried away by it. Georgie with her matter-of-factness and Pat with his familiarity with the route might not have been so susceptible to the influence, had their nerves not been already tingling from a recent shock. Agnes would always have been keenly alive to the influences of the hour and the situation. Now, cast down as she was from her spiritual heights and writhing in the depths of utter disappointment akin to despair, she was aware of a certain deadening, enthralling sense of novelty and of an overwhelming destiny which it was vain for her to resist. She felt delivered from the bondage of former habits and customs, and launched whether she would or not into an unknown life, as the train rushed on in the dim darkness of the summer night, and the boat ploughed its way over the unseen waters.

Possibly Mrs. Baldwin was also at once aided and stirred in the new crisis of her fate, by the same consciousness of mystery and of a fresh departure in her history. But when the boat arrived at Calais, and there was a gradual subsiding of the first natural excitement, unknown before to the three women—mother as well as daughters, of landing in a foreign country, amidst a little crowd of foreign men and women, in aspect and dress varying in sundry small but striking details from the aspect and dress of English sailors, custom-house officers, porters, fisher men and women, it was plain to see what a belated little party were there in the silvery morning light. They remained dumb in answer to the clamour of foreign tongues. They refused to be borne along by the small rush of their fellow-passengers, to swallow cups of

coffee, glasses of cogniac, and what food
they could find at the railway buffet.
The Baldwins sat huddled together, as it
seemed, in the compartment of the French
railway carriage to which Pat had taken
them, his mother on his arm, Agnes and
Georgie following close at their heels, as
if the sisters would be lost if they strayed
a hair's-breadth or lingered a second.
It was a singular proof how stunned and
prostrated the women were that speech
failed among the whole three. Nobody
asked, till Pat vouchsafed the information,
in what direction they were going, what
part of France, or it might be Italy or
Turkey, was to be their ultimate destination,
any more than those who did not know
demanded why they had come there.
Why, the whole framework of their ex-
istence had been shattered and its story
as it were brought to an end. True,
two of the travellers did know more or
less clearly, with the knowledge burnt

into their consciousness, the reason why this inconceivable transformation of their lives had come to pass within twenty-four hours. A third member of the company had had the veil partially torn from her eyes, enough, even while she vehemently shut them against the betraying light, to make her—high-spirited and courageous by original constitution—cling desperately to the rags of concealment which were yet left her, and dread with a sickening apprehension the stripping off of the last shred of bandage, the overthrow of the last tottering crumbling defence which ignorance could maintain against the withering shameful truth.

Georgie, the youngest and simplest of the group, had been taken by surprise without being further enlightened. But she was too wise and single-minded in her very simplicity not to put two and two together. She had been more with her mother than the others had been for years. To her unimaginative straight-forward mind, her mother's withdrawal from the world, her self-absorption and settled gloom, were more incomprehensible, unnatural and unhealthy, than they had ever appeared to Agnes, or even to Pat. Georgie had also been better acquainted with the episode of the old servant who haunted and harassed Mrs. Baldwin with his visits, and though the girl hated to cast blame on anybody, above all on her mother, she had arrived, by her unaided shrewdness, at the conclusion that Mrs. Baldwin was, or believed herself to be, in some odd manner, under a great obligation to Tweedside Johnnie, and thus far in his power. Georgie had not confided her opinion to Pat or Agnes, partly because she could not bear to reflect upon their mother, partly because, if she so much as hinted at such a disparaging idea to her sister, Agnes would not listen and would indignantly

silence the speaker. Georgie, ungifted
with that higher faculty which is apt to
deal for the most part inconveniently
and always dangerously with beloved ob-
jects, did not idolize her dearest friends.
Loving her mother honestly in her own
reasonable affectionate way, she yet saw
in her an erring mortal, who must always have been capable, like Georgie's
self for instance, of doing wrong and
foolish things in the course of her life.
In her clear-sighted acuteness, Georgie
was inclined to hold that her mother's
obstinate avoidance of social intercourse,
and the fashion in which she gave herself up to habitual depression, were in
themselves foolish and wrong. Still, with
filial instinct she shrank from the exposure of any error which her mother had
committed, while she was sure in her inno-
cence and kindness that it could not have
been a great error. It could only have been
some careless or reckless infringement of

rule and precedent, some offence against
the letter of the law, for which she was
thus, late in the day, by Tweedside
Johnnie's folly and faithlessness, doubtless called to account and persecuted.
Georgie's spirit rose in defence of her
mother.

Again, it was not altogether prostration of spirit which prevented Georgie
from cross-questioning Pat as to their
destination. Long ago Agnes had
appointed Georgie the family housekeeper
and purveyor for everybody's comfort
and well-being. She had rebelled against
the appointment as not giving a healthy,
well-disposed young woman, who was
not a genius certainly, enough to do in
the matter of contributing to the support
of the family, an obligation which, in
Pat's absence, Agnes had the audacity to
take on her slim shoulders and on the sharp
point of her pen. Though Georgie was
not a genius, she had a great ambition,

in the circumstances, to be self-support-
ing and useful ; but in spite of her protest
she took kindly to the office imposed
upon her, far more kindly than to the
*ignis fatuus* of becoming a great painter
which Agnes had also dangled before her
sister's eyes. The fact was, Georgie was
a born housekeeper, helpmeet and nurse,
instead of a painter ; she might perfectly
well have been both, but not being the
one she was certainly the other. At the
present moment she had it on her mind
that her mother must be cared for, and
Agnes seen to, and not allowed to
neglect her bodily wants. Pat might be
trusted to find out when he was tired,
hungry and thirsty, but neither of the
others could be left to themselves.
The crossing had been a good one, and
Mrs. Baldwin had as yet stood the
hurried journey very well, marvellously
so, considering the absolutely sedentary
life which she had led for many years.

But Georgie, watching her mother leaning
back in the corner of the carriage, with
her dull eyes half closed, a faint red
spot on each ashen check, her gloved
fingers occasionally moving with a little
involuntary action, as if they missed the
accustomed knitting, felt that she, Georgie,
must keep a vigilant eye on the elder
traveller, lest she should break down all
at once.    Pat, in his double capacity of
attentive son and learned physician, was
alive to the same possibility.   When he
had seen his charges seated in their
places, he ran back and fetched a waiter
with a tray of refreshments from the
buffet.   His mother took what he told
her to take, as she had risen and left
her home, at his bidding.  Georgie herself
was guilty of an appetite which she was
not ashamed to satisfy, just as Pat felt
bound to eat and drink without apology,
like a man.   But Agnes put everything
away from her as if food would choke

her. To the best of Georgie's belief, she had not swallowed enough to keep a sparrow in life for the last two days. This was a serious weight on Georgie's conscience, usurping her attention. It was in vain that she remonstrated in eager whispers : " You must take something, Agnes, now that you are here. You must avail yourself of what there is to eat ; it seems wholesome enough and not out of the way. It is quite silly of you not to force yourself to drink a cup of coffee and eat a bit of cake. What good will it do for you to make yourself ill ? "

Agnes only shook her head in a piteous negative ; her heart-sickness had made her body sick.

Georgie had to rest her faith on the broken reed of the biscuits which she took the precaution to buy and store, and the flask which Pat filled.

# CHAPTER II.

THERE was still nobody in the Baldwins' third-class carriage at so early an hour. They were at liberty to speak freely. "We are going to Normandy," Pat volunteered the information which nobody had sought. "I thought that quarter would do as well as any other, and it would not be too far for the mother."

Nobody spoke for a moment, nobody seemed to care where they went. Then Georgie, who was not in the habit of making quotations and indulging in far-fetched references—solemn or grotesque, in her excitement, worry about her mother and Agnes, and generally unsettled frame of mind, struck in with the doggrel:

"'There came four dukes from Normandy,
To court my daughter Jane.'

How fond you were of playing at that game when we were children, Agnes. I did not care for it, but you told long stories about each of the dukes, and about ' the pound ' which ' my daughter Jane ' carried away in her pocket for her dowry, which was not there when she returned." (The truth was, the Baldwins' proceeding in the present stage was not unlike a fantastic, incoherent play or game). "Normandy," repeated Georgie, who seemed doomed to be the speaker ; " we shall see the pippins *au naturel*, and as we shall be near Brittany I may take it for granted that we shall not want for butter."

" That's right, Georgie, make the best of things," answered Pat, with a laugh out of tune, to kill care as he would have said. " Quatr'eaux, for which we are bound, is not a show place, though it has a decent cathedral, I believe. It is not on the coast and it is not on a river of any consequence. though its name gives it the credit of four streams. It is out of the main line to places of greater importance and has been left to its own resources. It has not more than seven or eight thousand inhabitants, and they are principally engaged in the linen trade. I do not give you these valuable statistics from personal experience, but from Baedecker and a little hearsay evidence I chanced to pick up some months ago, which I have just called to mind. Let me tell you that Quatr'eaux has the distinction of being, beyond dispute, the cheapest little town in France. That is a consideration of paramount moment to us, since we, you two girls and I, must look out immediately for something to do, and make our earnings go as far as possible."

Pat had deliberately and advisedly been bringing round the conversation to the question of ways and means to which he was certain it would soon tend. In the hurry of starting, his family had, somewhat to his surprise, accepted his assurance that he was provided with money for the journey, without further question. But they would not long continue so passive, and the discussion of funds could not come too soon, particularly as it might divert reflection from more painful considerations. " A little money will come to us," Pat pursued the subject, still asserting his natural supremacy as the man in the group and for that conventional reason its leader. " There will be something from the sale of the furniture, which a broker is likely to take at a valuation." This was truly to scuttle the ship in their rear.

" The furniture ! " shrieked Georgie, taking the alarm ; " mother's furniture, the last remnant of what she brought from Brackengill ? Why, we shall have nothing to go back to. How could you take it upon you to dispose of mother's furniture without her knowledge and consent?"

Pat bent his brows. "It would have been impossible to bring it with us, Georgie. It would be still more foolish to have it sent after us. It will be time enough to think of what we have to go back to, when we are going back. Mother, you do not mind letting the furniture go?" he turned to her, with the same anxious, pitying, protecting gentleness with which he had behaved to her for the last fourteen hours.

"No," she said with an effort; "I have no wish ever to see it again."

Georgie was silenced. There was a rustle from Agnes's corner as she turned her face still farther out of sight. Even Pat was quenched for a moment. But it was part of his difficult duty to keep up his sisters' spirits as far as he could, and to launch their thoughts on a new train of calculation and enterprise. "There will be a little money sent over to us," he said again ; " but I think you will all agree with me that, even if we have to take the use of it in the meantime, it ought to be put back and told off, as soon as may be, to pay the loan which I have been forced to contract from a friend."

" Of course," said Georgie promptly.

Mrs. Baldwin bestirred herself to make some acquiescence. But all that Agnes did was to wince anew.

" At least we cannot be much worse off, in respect to worldly goods, than the generality of emigrants—than the old French *émigrés* were who came to England without a *sou*, with their lives in their hands, a century ago," resumed Pat, drumming with his fingers on the window pane by which he sat. " They contrived to make a living, so why should not we ? They had public sympathy on their sides, to be sure, while we cannot count on that," he wound up his sentence rapidly. " But,

I say, you girls," he began again with renewed animation, " I have been thinking that I have something in my favour— the fact that I have studied medicine in France, and taken a French degree. That ought to entitle me to practise my respectable calling of 'sawbones' in any town in France. I may not get a single patient, especially as we shall be wide of the track of English and American tourists, and national prejudice may be against me, but that is quite another matter. It is something to be qualified to work at one's lawful trade, whether the working be to profit or not. I might get a little dispensary work there as at Barnes, or I might take a turn in a chemist's shop ; it would be an honest enough shift, and I ain't proud, let us be thankful. As for you, Georgie, you were to witch the world with noble painting ; you shall attack the Cathedral : if it is comparatively small it is not hackneyed. You shall paint it

from every point of vantage.  It will
always be a genteel calling, you may
thank your stars; and some of the natives
ought to give you a few francs for your
sketches."

"They will not be such fools," said
Georgie ruefully; "but I have always had
an idea that I could teach drawing.  I
have had such good teaching, and plenty
of it, thanks to Agnes's too flattering
estimate of my abilities.  Though I have
never had much hope that the good teaching was not thrown away upon me, it
might enable me to get drawing pupils;
and I know English fairly—of course.
Mother pinched herself to provide us with
tolerable governesses, and I could undertake
to impart the rudiments of my mother-
tongue.  I wish I had not heard, or that
there was no foundation for the report,
which represented the mass of little French
girls as getting their education in convents."

The young Baldwins had been brought

up so far to earn their living ; but to set about it as two of them now proposed, in a moment, in a strange place, sounded very like a wild-goose chase. Both Pat and Georgie were too quick-witted not to be aware of the huge obstacles to their success, which, on the whole, they felt it better to ignore.

Pat's next suggestion had a more reasonable, feasible ring about it. " As for Agnes," said Pat, " she will be able to concoct her romances as well in France as in England, at Quatr'eaux as at Barnes. They will have a new setting, that is all. Publishers are within reach of the post. Let us be thankful Agnes has elected to be our bread-winner for months past ; she must hold on a little longer till Georgie and I find a footing. Happily for everybody our move is, if anything, in her favour, opening up for her pen fresh fields and pastures new and that style of thing. It will make no further difference to her."

How strange Pat's speech sounded!
He did not mean to be unkind, far from
it.    He was paying Agnes the highest
compliment he knew of, with gratifying
sincerity and really warm affectionateness.
He was turning to her with a half-stifled
sigh of relief, as still the mainstay of the
family, the member whose resources, now
as ever, could be depended upon.    Irony
or cruelty was the very last thing he was
thinking of, yet Agnes felt as if she were
mocked and taunted.    Would the events of
to-day and yesterday make no difference
to her?    What did the speaker take her
for?    She remembered with a pang that she
had asked the same question of Sam Scrope.
But could Georgie and Pat not guess that
the events of to-day and yesterday had
made all the difference in the world to her?
With her heart wrung, her faith slain,
her peace poisoned, how could her imagina-
tion escape the universal blight which had
fallen upon her world?    Oh! how little

they understood, even while they shared
in this awful calamity, what it was to
her. How could they be beginning
already to look forward and make plans?
She smiled a faint woe-begone smile and
slightly shook her head. Yet she did
not wish to fail them, or to dispirit the
very persons whom she had been wont
to stimulate and support. She tried to say
something which would meet the circumstances. "I do not know about writing.
It is not a thing which can really be taken
up anywhere, any day, in any circumstances—unless in the case of an Anthony
Trollope, in circumstances which have
no similarity to mine. It is a faculty
which, I fancy, may perish in an instant.
Invention and the root of invention both
dying at a stroke. They do sometimes,
and I have often wondered that it does
not happen oftener. But that is not to
say I shall not find work of some kind.
I can teach as well as Georgie, if you leave

out drawing. I am young and strong; I shall not fare worse than my neighbours."

Agnes was stopped by a low groan from her mother, who had been listening and glancing at her. Mrs. Baldwin sat up, and the face which had looked so frozen in its stony grief commenced to melt and quiver. She wrung her gloved hands impotently. " Oh ! my poor children, I am to be such a trouble to you," she moaned ; " I thought to shield you, and I shall be your bane. I shall spoil Pat and Georgie's prospects and I shall blast Agnes's bright career. Think of it ! I shall blast the career of my good and gifted child, who has done so much for me and all her kindred. If you could only find some cheap, obscure hole where I could hide out of sight and pass away when God's time came, without doing you any more injury, I should be thankful—glad ; I should count myself better off than I deserve to be. I dare not anticipate God's time—that would only bring down more sin and disgrace," she cried a little wildly; "but it cannot be long now—oh! it cannot be much longer, and you need not wait for that. You may all go back *home* at once; Pat will find a practice; and Georgie will keep house for him or get teaching without difficulty in her own country; and Agnes can write her books, her delightful stories, which the best judges have praised and augured highly from, which will make so many toiling, suffering people wiser and better, while she herself grows rich and famous as she deserves to do. And I, if I live to hear it, will rejoice. Am I not her mother in my misery—the mother of all you children?"

The listeners were taken by surprise. It was so unheard of for their mother to rouse herself and share in their discussions, to give as it were a personal revelation of herself, even to make so long a speech. Sad and standing apart as they had always known her, letting them go their own way and interfering little with them, she had never conveyed to them the idea of being set aside, as far as they were concerned ; she had not been regarded either by herself or them as unfit to claim the pre-eminence which she had voluntarily resigned. She had been a proud, dignified woman naturally, and the very manner in which she had—whatever sorrow she endured, sufficed for herself, wrapping herself up in an impenetrable reserve, had lent her a kind of melancholy exaltation, as far removed from weakness and worthlessness as from cheerfulness. It was inexpressibly pitiful to her children to have her thus abase herself before them.

"Hush ! mother," said Pat, speaking with the impatience, well-nigh resentment, under a show of which a man is fain to mask a very different emotion.

" Of course you are my charge, say no more about it."

" Oh ! what nonsense, mother," chimed in Georgie, and then it was on the tip of her honest tongue to implore : " But tell us all about it ; trust us, your children, and it will be better for you and everybody." But a warning glance from Pat stopped her. This was no time or place to press for her mother's confidence. Instead, she continued her rallying tone while, as she did so, she employed one of those terms of endearment which were not frequent in the Baldwins' mouths. " Dear, how could you imagine that we should leave you behind us ? Why, we should not know ourselves without you."

Agnes's tongue clave to the roof of her mouth, while her mother looked at her in an agony of expectation. More even than on her only son, Mrs. Baldwin's heart had been set on her elder daughter. The girl's untiring energy, her dauntless

courage, her unbounded faith, the touch
of genius which marked her out from
other girls, had fascinated and held fast
her mother's tenderest, strongest affections;
she had been proud of Agnes from her
childhood. The one ray of happiness,
of hopeful association with the outer
world, which Mrs. Baldwin had allowed
herself to retain was in watching Agnes's
progress as an author and in listening
to her songs. The mother had read and
re-read every line of her daughter's which
had appeared in print, and it need hardly
be added that, though a woman of good
judgment originally, she had exaggerated
their merit and importance; she had
learned to attach an undue weight to
everything Agnes said and did, or failed
to say and do.

The conviction in Mrs. Baldwin's mind
that she had been made to work serious,
deadly harm to Agnes, so that the mother
had killed at one fell blow the daughter's

belief in human goodness and what had hitherto been her passionate, reverent love for her mother, was more bitter than death to Mrs. Baldwin. It constituted a punishment which, though she had foreseen something of the kind coming, and cowered in abject fear of its approach all these years, now that it was upon her, proved worse than she had been able to conceive, harder almost than she could bear.

Quatr'eaux was not unlike many French and a few English towns of its size. The Cathedral with its chapels and towers, fretwork and pinnacles—the solitary architectural boast of the place, stood in the middle of the older part of the town, the centre of a labyrinth of old-fashioned, narrow, somewhat squalid streets of tall houses with high-pitched roofs. There was a tolerably quaint market-place among the houses, presided over by the statue of a mediæval bishop of Quatr'eaux, who wore a breast-plate instead of a lace

robe and held a drawn sword in the room
of a crozier. In spite of the breast-plate
and sword of the church militant, it was said
that he had been hunted from his bishopric
and narrowly escaped murder at the
hands of the revolted wolfish sheep of
his fold. In this provincial market, regu-
lated by the mayor, who enforced strict
primitive market laws of buying and
selling, were stalls of flowers and fruit,
interspersed with stalls of yard-long French
bread, meat and poultry cut and trussed
French fashion, shoes and *sabots*, earthen-
ware *pots-au-feu* and pipkins, and yet
other stalls which vindicated the ecclesias-
tical side of the town. These last displayed
long rows of what Georgie at first sight
cried were "images" of saints or monks
and nuns, with halo-encircled or hooded
and cowled heads, relieved against little
plantations of floridly carved and gilded
crucifixes, garlanded with rosaries.

On three sides of the town stretched

the suburbs of semi-genteel and wholly
genteel modern terraces and squares and
villa-like houses, of which the *portes
cochères* and the *jalousies* were the most
conspicuous attributes.  These formed the
residences of the richer linen manufacturers and professional men of Quatr'eaux.
On the fourth side of the town, though
there was no river to speak of and all
the travelling and traffic of the inhabitants were maintained by diligences and
carriers' carts communicating with the
terminus of a branch line of railway,
there still remained one of the minor
streams and brooklets of which there had
apparently once been four.  The sole
survivor had much the look of a more
or less stagnant ditch encircling this
quarter of the town.  Beyond the trick-
ling channels and green pools lay a little
bit of a great dark changeless forest.
The knowledge of its vicinity stirred the
pulses, though in reality there was not

even a tree of respectable size to be seen,
simply a belt of brushwood with a spindly
young elm or poplar rising at intervals
to break the monotony, because the townspeople of Quatr'eaux had the right of
bringing in firewood from the forest.  But
Pat was prepared to say there was a
veritable forest, and that if you pursued
any of its woodland paths long enough
you would find the scene stately and
solemn, lonesome, bewildering and weird,
as all true forests are.  Within the
memory of living men, not merely rabbits,
hares, roebuck, and foxes in abundance,
but white-fanged wolves had emerged in
hard winters from its dim recesses.  The
wedge of forest beyond the brooklet, so
lazy and overgrown with water-ranunculus
that the washerwomen could not beat
their linen white in its scanty waters,
was the most foreign, the nearest to a
poetic element in Quatr'eaux.  There had
been a time when it would have entranced

Agnes, when it would have been invaluable to her fancy like a gold mine to a hunter after the precious metal; but when she arrived in the town she was so sorely borne down by undreamt-of misfortune, so nearly broken-hearted, that she did not notice the beginning of the woodland wilderness.

Pat scarcely gave the weary women time to rest in the old inn near the Cathedral, where there were *garçons* for waiting-maids, before he hurried them into the greater privacy of quiet lodgings in a side street. Pat's familiarity with colloquial French was far removed from the girls' insular schoolroom acquaintance with the language, which they would have brought forward, had they been without him, with justifiable dubiousness and shyness. His former stay in Paris stood him and his family in good stead, in more ways than one, though he had little guessed to what use it would be pat. He had found no difficulty in looking up and securing the modest little suite of rooms in a locality not too airless for life to be lived in them, which was all that he ventured to engage. The apartments were above the shop of a man-milliner and his wife, who made various lively gestures and grimaces in signifying that the band-box rooms were not only all they should be, the *famille anglaise* would find them charming, ravishing, beyond any *étage* they had ever known, and a ridiculous bagatelle where expense was in question. The man-milliner was prepared with gay politeness to act as *concierge*, madame his wife would see that the cooking, serving and scouring were done to a wish by old Suzanne, their own incomparable, trustworthy domestic.

When Pat had learnt for himself that the polished wooden floors, the brilliant cretonne curtains, the gorgeous rugs, the high-piled beds, the superabundance of

glass and gilding were intact and reason-
ably clean, he was satisfied. What did
it matter that the most imposing article of
furniture in the sitting-room was a glit-
tering steel stove, and that its ornaments
consisted of one of the "images" which
Georgie's rampant Protestantism objected
to—that of *Marguerite Marie à la Coque*
on a small pedestal above the chimney-
piece—a rosary blessed by his Holiness
the Pope suspended on a wall opposite,
and on one of the little side tables, piles
on piles of books of French fashions, more
frivolous, one was tempted to suppose,
than their English copies.

In this incongruous little room the
women of the party were destined to
receive a new shock. Pat thought fit to
mention his name and calling to his
landlord, and Georgie, for one, could not
believe her ears when she found that her
brother had forgotten his surname though
not his calling. With a heightened colour,

but with perfect distinctness, he described himself as " Dr. Patrick Raimes," not " Dr. Patrick Baldwin." Why, " Raimes," to which poor Pat was clinging desperately, was but a fragment of his name, his middle name and not his surname. He was giving it in the infatuation which causes men to whom lying is strange, to hold on by a shred of the truth, though they are sensible that it is not in fact the truth, and will be falsely interpreted, nay, that the poor subterfuge may serve to undo their efforts, and betray what the speakers are struggling to conceal.

" Pat !" cried Georgie impulsively and stopped ; frightened by the look on his face, she turned to her mother, whose lips fell apart as she gasped for breath. Georgie glanced at Agnes ; she seemed fit to sink into the ground with shame and misery. Oh ! the degradation of a feigned name, a disguised personality, the glib resource of rogues and vagabonds. Georgie read the truth in her sister's face and was startled and staggered; she grew scarlet and hung her head. The next moment she recalled that it might be a necessary precaution in their strange position, which was yet to be accounted for. Pat must feel bound to take the precaution, yet he had not the appearance of a fugitive from law and justice, or of a swindler of his neighbours, in taking it. It was with a defiant rather than a furtive glance around that he uttered what was neither more nor less than an assumed name.

If Pat was "Dr. Raimes," then, to maintain the harmony of his narrative without elaborate mis-statements, which Georgie could not help calling "more lies," she and Agnes and their mother must all be Raimeses, though the women could not even claim the title as a middle name. There was no actual sin, unless it lay in incurring a subtle flavour of dis-honesty from an intent to deceive, in

borrowing a name, or dropping it in part,
or changing it by the omission of a syl-
lable or a letter. What was in a name?
People altered their names every day, from
vanity, from whim, in order to secure the
succession to a fortune. Might not innocent people take the same liberty from
some mysterious obligation which concerned
the welfare of those near and dear to
them? It was awkward, of course, and
disturbing to one's dignity to be thus
verbally masquerading and losing one's
nominal identity; what was a great deal
worse, it was not true : that was the sum
and substance of the obnoxious offence
in Georgie's eyes, but it had to be done
sometimes, without doubt. Surely Agnes
was exaggerating when she made so much
of it—Agnes, who had taken a *nom de
plume* and called herself as an author
" Judith Westmoreland " without the
smallest scruple. They had all laughed
at the disguise, the motive of which was

very different certainly, though Georgie had pointed out from the first that there might be people, postmen and handmaids like Selina, who would not recognize the difference. Agnes could not see their difficulty. Yet it was Agnes who kept moaning and muttering in the middle of the night, when she thought nobody heard her, "Oh, poor Pat and Georgie! If it had fallen on me alone, if I could have saved them, I might have borne it better. But it is hard that their fair fame should be breathed upon by a stale, base device which may be remembered against them all through their lives, that they should ever be pointed out as a pair who had to skulk under an alias! Mother, mother, what have you done?"

# CHAPTER III.

THE question, "What had Mrs. Baldwin
done?" could not remain unanswered
much longer. Agnes's torturing doubts
and suspicions, Georgie's practical common
sense, alike demanded an explanation.
What happened took place on the evening of the first Sunday which the family
spent at Quatr'eaux, where they arrived
on a Friday. The intervening Saturday
had been passed in a futile effort to
settle down where all were so much out
of their element. Pat had walked about
pioneering Georgie to the market and the
nearest shops, and interpreting between her
and the natives. Georgie had unpacked
as far as it was possible, after she discovered to her dismay that there were only

the smallest cupboards and the tiniest chests of drawers in which to bestow three grown-up women's entire suits of wearing apparel, for all the four seasons. She had further exerted herself in the most praiseworthy manner to lend a habitable, homelike air, to what were to her the gimcrack Frenchified rooms. Happy Georgie, who could occupy and forget herself thus profitably.

Agnes had sought to follow Georgie's example as if she were in a dream and did not really know what she did, so that every few minutes she, who had never owned to fatigue, who had been so endless in resource, was fain to fall into a seat, fold her hands in weary wretchedness and look helplessly to Georgie in order to gather what she, Agnes, was to do next.

Mrs. Baldwin sat motionless by the unlit stove, as she had been accustomed to sit by the fire generally kept burning for her benefit, even in the summer time, in the drawing-room at Barnes. She never touched the piece of knitting which Georgie had rather ostentatiously brought in and placed at her mother's elbow. Mrs. Baldwin hardly looked up at all the novelty around her, unless when Agnes went out and in, and then the mother followed the daughter with eyes in whose depths were fathomless depreca-tion and longing.

Then came Sunday with another variety of strangeness of aspect. All the world of Quatr'eaux, as it seemed to the Bald-wins, went early to confession and mass, and then spread themselves abroad, im-partially, for the purpose of enjoying themselves. The streets were full of people in holiday attire, country people as well as townspeople, come in for their weekly holiday. The restaurants and the wine shops were doing a brisk trade. As the season was summer, little tables were grouped under the awnings for the accommodation of men who read the newspapers, argued vociferously, drank harmless drinks, smoked and played dominoes. So far as posters could proclaim the fact, the night was going to be a gala one at the little theatre.

There was no English church in a town where few English were to be seen. The Baldwins talked of seeking out "the Temple," where, as they understood, the modern representatives of the old Huguenots continued to worship in more than Puritan plainness and sombreness; but the strangers had not the spirit to make the move to-day.

As the afternoon wore on to evening, a certain hush fell on the merry-makers without, and a corresponding stillness descended on the family party within; even Pat, who had been fidgeting about after the manner of a young man with nothing to do, gradually sank down into a seat in a window, and lying back, with his arms folded above his head—an old attitude of his, listlessly contemplated the passers-by.

Georgie, who was the soul of orderly duty, suddenly proposed to read aloud for the edification of the company. "It will give us more of the feeling of a Sunday, don't you think?" she suggested. "It seems too queer and Bohemian to have no church, no service, and all that stir in the street. I declare there is a brass band coming; I must wait till it is gone."

As nobody objected, Georgie read the evening lessons, apparently with satisfaction to others as well as to herself, for when she closed her prayer-book, Mrs. Baldwin asked her abruptly to read a chapter in the Bible, naming the 5th chapter of Acts. Georgie turned it up obediently. "Oh, it is such a dismal chapter," she made a little protest when she saw what she was to read.

"Read it," said Mrs. Baldwin briefly.

18—2

Georgie, unacquainted with any reason why she should not comply, save what had to do with a natural shrinking from the sad stern story of a traitor and traitress, with their terrible doom following hard on the heels of their transgression, did as she was bid. After she had read to the 11th verse, "And great fear came upon all the church and upon as many as heard these things," Mrs. Baldwin again interposed.

"That will do, Georgie," her mother said in a low tone. She added in a higher key, "Now I must speak to you, children, once and for all. I must tell you my temptation and my sin, how I lied like Sapphira and committed a fraud. Oh, God! If I could but put the memory away from me for ever."

It was as if a bombshell had fallen into the quiet room, though all present had been waiting, almost wishing, for such an opening. Pat had let his arms drop

during the reading; he now sat bolt upright and opened his mouth to keep his
mother from saying another word. But
on second thoughts he forbore. " Better
it should come from herself after all, poor
woman; better for her and for everybody,"
he reasoned to himself.

Georgie sat aghast with the Bible on
her knee and her finger inadvertently
pointed to the words, "and great fear came
upon all."

Agnes shivered and drew as much as
she could out of sight behind the cretonne
hangings.

Mrs. Baldwin did not flinch from the
task she had undertaken. She sat in the
midst of them in her widow's weeds, and
lifted up her pale face to meet their shrinking gaze.

" I must begin at the beginning," she
said, " or you will not be able to understand me, or to make allowance for me,
if there is any allowance to be made. I

did not marry your father for love. My
father's family were poor, though well-
born, and in my young days it was not
held creditable for a gentlewoman to work
for her living, as many people now hold
it to be. Girls were not glad and proud
to do it, as I think the wisest and best of
them are in your generation. Besides, I
could not have done it; my accomplish-
ments were of the flimsiest description. I
had been taught nothing useful and nothing
thoroughly, for it was supposed that I had
not a strong constitution. Marriage was
my one resource, as it was of most girls
like me. At least I broke no vows and
played no man false, in order to marry
Dick Baldwin. It was all the other way.
I mean a man had broken his vows to me
and played me false—but I do not wish
to rake up the ashes of a past wrong,
they are nothing but dead ashes to-day,"
she declared in the same dreary monotone
in which she had first spoken, which she

preserved for the most part throughout her statement. " Your father knew that I had no heart to give him, yet he was willing to make me his wife, and I consented since he did not ask or desire much from me ; I do not think it was in his nature. He liked my person, approved of my manners, and fancied that I should discharge the duties of the mistress of his establishment as well as most women. I married him in order to secure a provision and shelter for the years which were to come. I never doubted that he knew it and did not object to the terms of our contract. He never required more from me than I gave him as his due ; he never accused me of failing him. We were not at all alike in character and tastes ; we were not much together except in company. We fell apart naturally ; but there was no wrangling or quarelling between us, such as one might have found between more closely-attached couples, or couples that have begun their wedded life more closely attached. Then God sent us children, little as we might seem to deserve them, and I thought all was going to be made up to me ; not that I dreamt the children would draw my husband and me more closely together. It is commonly held that it is so, and it may be true in some cases. But your father was not fond of children. He had a certain pride and pleasure in you, I will not deny that, especially in Pat as his son and heir. I used to think his preference for the boy was unjust to Agnes, who was the first-born, and was always very fond of her father."

"Don't, mother, don't !" cried Agnes passionately. It felt like being guilty of treason to hear the amount of her dead father's love for her weighed against her deserts and found wanting. She put up her trembling hands as if to stop her ears, and the signet ring would have slipped from her finger had she not caught it and

held it fast. Her mother's heavy sigh
was the only notice which she took of the
interruption.

" Your father left you very much to
me, who could not have too much of you.
I was happy then, yes, I can honestly say
I was happy, when you were all young,"
she said with a softening of her mask
of a face and one yearning backward look,
as if from wintry skies, at the perished
summer of her life. " Then your father's
affairs fell into disorder," she began again
with dogged resolution. " The great firm
in which he was a partner were in straits,
and I knew it. I began to fear, night
and day, not that I should be robbed of
the safety, ease and luxury which I had
bought at the highest price I could pay,
but that you, my children, whom I had
loved better than myself—I can say that
also, after I have disgraced and ruined
you—whom I had born as I believed to
a liberal competence, if not to vast wealth,

to the bright and bountiful lot of those who are regarded as the favourites of fortune, because they are independent of her smiles and frowns—should be cast on the charity of a cold world, driven to struggle and fight for a bare subsistence, very likely trampled down in the fight. It half maddened me to think of that. I had looked forward to such a different destiny for you. Yet I could spare pity for your poor father; I think I was never so near caring for him as when I saw him beaten by cruel odds, borne down by the terrible unrelieved pressure. He was soon beyond my pity—so far as desiring it or prizing it went. He had been fast growing old before the full weight of his misfortunes came upon him, and it turned the balance; he became imbecile where he had before been infirm. My horror was that, in this state, with his partners calling on him to produce his accounts, and urging an examination into the affairs of the firm, he would commit some irretrievable blunder, condemn himself far beyond truth and reason, and deprive you, in your ignorance and helplessness, of the little that was likely to be left for you and me. Then I did wish he might die first. I began to pray and long for the death which the doctors had said could not be delayed for many weeks," she ended with a look of affright and speaking in a low choked voice.

Not a sound could be heard in the little room. It was as if the appalled audience held their breath, in the growing stillness of the summer evening, with the peace and solemnity of their recent Sunday reading still lingering in the air. Any sound which reached the listeners' ears from the world without was as the last echoes of the gaiety of the people's holiday. It had struck the English spectators as frivolous, almost profane, but it now occurred to them that it was certainly as domestic as it had been public. For the larger proportion of the company returning from their visiting and pleasure-seeking consisted of family groups, father, mother and children of all ages, still smart and cheery, patient and enduring in their weariness.

"It was just at this season of the year," went on Mrs. Baldwin, though her throat was dry and she had to make an evident effort to keep calm, "on a beautiful morning in early summer, that Tweedside Jeannie came and called me. I was in the nursery, where I had elected to sleep, since it was not thought well that I should be constantly, night as well as day, watching by your father. Jeannie ought to have been with him that night. She best knew how she fulfilled her trust. She and her husband were old servants of your father's, who had been with him when I married him, whom he always held in great esteem. Jeannie was understood to have skill and experience as a nurse in the days when trained nurses were not

so common as you may find them now.
Though your father was so hopelessly ill
he was not confined to bed, not even to
his chair. He could walk abroad a little
in a feeble way, which rendered it the
more necessary that he should be carefully
watched, lest he should stray out of doors
at an unseasonable hour, or stumble and
fall, so doing himself harm. His bedroom
was on the ground floor, so that he
might the more easily get into the open
air. The bedroom opened from the
library, which had a door—half door, half
window—that led by two or three steps to
a side lawn—the elder of you three may
remember it. Your father must have
been left alone early that morning, and
he had managed to rise, put on his dressing-gown and wander out as he was fond
of doing. He had met nobody, or if he
had, they had not accosted him and
sought to get him back to the house.
For Jeannie took me, not to his room,

but by the other door into the library,
and out through the side door on to the
lawn, towards the shrubbery, in which
was the pond. All she would say was
that something had happened and I must
come quickly to tell what was to be done.
And there, when we passed the weeping
ash which closed in the vista, I could see
that the boat which was used on the
pond had been unmoored and pulled up,
not to the regular landing-place, but to
the turf bank which sloped up from the
water. Straggling rays of the sun were
piercing their way through such a mist as
we often have on a fine morning, and were
falling on torn sedges and trodden-down
grass, on the oars flung about anywhere,
on Tweedside Johnnie standing as if he
were bereft of his senses, looking down
fixedly at a dripping figure in wet, dis-
ordered clothes, lying motionless at his
feet. The figure was that of my husband,
I saw it in a moment, and I knew by

the swollen discoloured look of the face, the glassiness of the wide-open eyes, and the purple rings round the nails of the hand, thrown across his breast, that my prayers had been heard : he was dead, drowned, gone beyond his friends' and enemies' reproaches and cross-question-ings."

"Oh, mother ! what a terrible shock for you," cried Georgie impetuously.

"But you could not help it," cried Agnes eagerly ; "it was none of your doing," she stopped short in an instant. What was she saying ? Yet Sam Scrope had been mistaken. Oh, thank God for it ; whatever the wrong done, there had been no deliberate little neglect, no in-human small act, on a mad impulse, in an hour of desperation, committed against a defenceless old man.

"Be quiet, Georgie," said Pat authori-tatively, and Agnes again shrank back, while her mother once more took up

her ghastly tale as if it were but half
told.

"I do not know how soon Jeannie
missed him from his room, or how she
and her husband traced him to the pond.
I was only told that Johnnie saw the
body in the water, not far from the
edge, got out the boat and succeeded
in dragging the corpse in and bringing
it to the bank. The man and woman
did not know, nobody ever will know till
God's judgment-day, whether your father,
wandering, he knew not whither, though
by a familiar pathway, stumbled and fell
into the water, without any possibility of
regaining his footing, which might very
well be, or whether a gleam of light and
intelligence had shot across his clouded
bewildered brain, and seeing no way out
of the labyrinth in which he found himself he thought to end it, God forsaken,
by the first means he could command, by
the water at hand. In the middle of my

horror I had a vivid impression of a new misfortune to my poor children : you would be thenceforth branded as the children of a suicide ; nobody would doubt that your father had taken his life—more than that, with the usual charity of the world, the public would be convinced that he had not committed the crime without sufficient cause. The worst charges against him must be regarded as proven, by his own desperate act, from that day forward."

# CHAPTER IV.

## THE COST OF A LIE.

"I THINK it was the woman Jeannie who first made a suggestion," proceeded Mrs. Baldwin in the silence which still prevailed. "I had not reproached her— how could I? I knew I had tried to do my duty, but if I had loved him, should I have been so long absent from his side, in the circumstances? She took the first word, because she was the craftier, as well as by far the bolder of the pair, though she was the woman and he the man. Could we not hush up the accident, as she called it, take the master back to his room, say we had found him dead, which was true in the main, and stop all idle talk? I cannot tell if she was aware of all the consequences of

such a step, but it darted across my
mind, in an instant, that your father's
life had been insured for a considerable
sum, at the time of our marriage, on my
behalf and for the benefit of any children
born of the marriage. I had reason to
believe that he had paid the premiums
up to the last which was due. If it
were known that he had not died a
natural death, while there was a strong
presumption that he had put away himself, the life insurance which he had kept
up all these years would be forfeited, and
the money he had spent on it lost.
On the other hand, if it could be made
to seem that he had died of a complica-
tion of natural diseases, as the doctors
had confidently asserted he would before
very long, the insurance money would be
saved, and would furnish a respectable
provision for you and me, such as your
father had destined for us from the first.
Nobody would be injured, as it appeared

to me, for had not your poor father paid the required amount punctually for a period of years? His reputation would be spared the last total eclipse, and who could tell, then or ever, whether he had really meant to take his life? You, his innocent children, would be delivered from inheriting any part of the crowning stigma he had unhappily incurred. As for the insurance company, it was a company and not an individual. The payment would be spread over so many members that nobody in particular would feel it. The disbursement was only discharging a just debt to us, by returning the money which Mr. Baldwin had paid up faithfully by degrees. A company, according to our north country saying, has a 'broad back,' while the sum, the withdrawal of which from their capital would be of so little consequence to a body of men, made all the difference between sufficiency and penury to you and me.

For I was too unacquainted with business
to reckon beforehand on the small allowance which your father's firm afterwards
granted to us, till their affairs were settled.
I tell you," she added a little wildly,
"the birds began to sing as I stood
there thinking, in a tempest of doubt,
and it sounded, even with that wreck of
humanity under my eyes, as if the
storm of adversity might blow by, and
the world be a pleasant place to us once
more. I may have been utterly heartless, but I was not an old woman then
—I felt life and health coursing in my
veins. I had you, my darlings, and I
had taken such delight in surrounding
you hitherto with all bright and happy
surroundings. It seemed grossly unfair
that you and I should be stripped and
condemned to suffer for no fault of yours
or mine. No harm to speak of would
be done to any living creature by the
deception which should procure our re-

prieve. Need I say that I yielded to the temptation? We—the woman Jeannie and I—arranged it all between us, Jeannie still taking the initiative, for I was much shaken and confused, and besides had never been quick at stratagems. It was still very early, too early we considered for any of the servants to be about, though perhaps we were mistaken in that and in some other conclusions. If we waited a little longer there would be the still greater security of everybody's being gone to breakfast. Your father was a little light-made man like Pat, and worn by sickness. Tweedside Johnnie, though short was thick-set, long-armed and muscular, and his wife was able-bodied. It was not difficult for them to do what they did. He brought out by the library door a small wicker-work couch on which I used to lie down in the bed-room, and the man and woman carried the body, wrapped in the dressing-gown and laid on the couch, through the library back to the bedroom. There they undressed it, put on such a night-dress as your father had worn, removed the wet clothes, and gave the alarm."

Mrs. Baldwin supplied the details with a kind of dull matter-of-factness that was in itself a shock to the listeners, while it was simply the result of much solitary brooding over the ghastly incident, until it had grown strangely familiar to her. " If by some chance the couple had met anybody on their way," she went on to explain, " they had but to tell what had actually befallen their master, and I should have come forward and given my evidence to clear them. What could be more natural and excusable than that we should have tried to stifle the miserable facts attendant on my husband's end ? I was his widow, and they were his old confidential servants ; such concealments are looked upon as quite pardonable, well-nigh sacred. They are practised, when they are possible, by the most devoted relatives and friends. Oh, why should I recall all the insidious arguments for a wicked deed?" Mrs. Baldwin suddenly broke off, her calmness deserting her, as she threw out her gaunt arms for an instant, as if to thrust away any specious palliative of her offence, and then pressed them against her heaving breast. "I lent myself to a heartless lie, a cunning fraud, and truly I had not long to wait for my reward. Retribution came upon me at once. Before the necessary forms could be complied with, and we had touched a farthing of the money for which your father's life was insured, the insurance company became bankrupt, and every penny which might have been ill-gotten gear, if it had come to us, was lost, and the chief inducement to the cheat swept away. The punishment

might have been just, but it was hard,
as the ways of a transgressor are said to
be—not the less so that I have never had
an hour's peace since I betrayed the
cause of truth and honesty, and of all
natural feeling. We were not reduced to
such poverty as I had dreaded while my
children were still young. The affairs of
the firm with which your father was con-
nected turned out a little better than was
anticipated. There were obligations on
the remaining partners which I had not
understood, or else they were sufficiently
moved by your father's death to make
us an allowance while the estate lasted.
What does it signify which was the reason?
I only wish to say that it was not be-
reavement or poverty which made my life
bitter and robbed it of all rest? it was
my loss of self-respect, the accusing voice
of my conscience, the abject terror of
being discovered in what I had done.
And I was continually harassed by the

ignorant scheming pair whose tool I had been, quite as much as they had been my tools. But should I fling the blame on them? They knew little better. They acted as might have been expected of them. One of them—the survivor, the passive instrument in the hands of the coarser, stronger nature—has been driven out of his wits by superstitious terror working on the weakness of age. Their whole principles, standards and position rendered them less accountable than I was," she ended, with a despairing candour.

Again there was dead silence for a moment, which Pat broke, as he rose up and came and stood by his mother. "It is all over so far as you are concerned, I trust," he said brokenly and soothingly. "You are here with us, out of the reach of everybody who knows, and you will not be followed, though there has been a show of examining into the case. Think no

more of it; you have rued and suffered
for it enough, God knows. We'll never
speak of it again, so help us. It was an
awful temptation for you, no doubt, and
it is not for us, in any light, to be your
judges. It is for us to take care of you
and comfort you as far as we can."

"God bless you, Pat," said his mother
faintly.

" Yes," chimed in Georgie, pushing back
her hair from her face, as if to put away
the grim picture which had been conjured
up before her. While she spoke she rose
up hastily in the gathering twilight, came
towards Mrs. Baldwin, and put her hand
gently on the other's shoulder. " Poor
mother ! you were hard beset and taken
unawares ; you cared so much for your
children, who were not able to help you
then, who were only a burden to you.
We all do wrong many a time, and often
without the cruel alternative which was
presented to you. Mother, do not think

of the terrible time again.   As Pat says,
it is all over and done with; you are
far away from it all.   We are around
you."

Agnes still cowered as if paralyzed in
her corner.   It was to her that her mother
turned with an agonized appeal.  " Agnes,"
Mrs. Baldwin cried with a great and
bitter cry, " can you not forgive me?
Will you never love me again ?"

"I ?   I will try, mother.   Oh, forgive
me—it is for you to forgive, not for me,"
moaned poor Agnes with parched lips,
and her throat swelling as if it would
suffocate her.   But when she would have
risen and gone to her mother as Pat and
Georgie had done, something held her
back as with the grip of a vice.   This
was not the mother whom Agnes had
known and loved, this strange woman
who had told with lips which had not
failed, and a voice that had not died away
in shame, the tale of her falsehood and

degradation. The mother Agnes Baldwin
had adored was a devoted, unworldly
woman, living under the shadow of a
great sorrow—so sacred in its character
that its very presence—while it had subdued, had exalted the atmosphere of the
house in which she dwelt. This was a
woman who had shrunk in craven fear,
under the shadow of a base sin and the
chance of its detection, whose neighbourhood could bring no blessing with it,
either for herself or others. She had been
cold-blooded and calculating from the beginning. She had sold herself to a loveless marriage and a luxurious home, secure
and safe from change ; she had so dreaded
poverty for herself and her children that
she had preferred to stain herself with the
guilt of a common liar and thief.

It was well-nigh incredible to Agnes
that any woman should so have quailed
and sunk before the bare anticipation of
that poverty which Agnes, in her tender

girlhood, had defied and scorned, which she had taken a high-hearted pleasure in holding at bay, and fighting off, in a hand-to-hand fight, by her unaided exertions. It was not to be thought that she could realize that there was another poverty infinitely more grievous than any she had known, which she had encountered at once so loftily and lightly in the gifts of her youth, health, strength, and unusual mental endowments. What had she experienced of the bondage of debt, the pinch of absolute want, the misery of witnessing the sufferings of her nearest and dearest without the power of helping them? And what she had not seen she could not in this instance conceive. This mother of hers who was not her mother, had come under the iron arm of the law which was a protection against evil-doers. She had become a partner in a palpable and singularly heartless fraud, with two such despicable domestic traitors as Tweedside

Johnnie and his wife, and from that date the unhappy woman had passed into their power, and become the bond slave of her servants.

The story was not so horrible as Sam Scrope had surmised when Agnes spurned his surmises, but it was more sordid, more repellant in its callous mercenariness. Agnes's righteous soul, righteous overmuch, sickened at the audacious unrighteousness of the deed.

"There must be no more of this," Pat was enjoining as he struck a light. He was speaking in the new authoritative tones, which he had only begun to exercise lately, of the natural protector and champion of the women around him. "It is idle and worse than useless to dwell on what had much better be forgotten. Mother, you will not be able to sleep tonight. Agnes, you are the last woman I should have threatened with hysterics, but if you do not take care I shall not war-

rant you against the complaint. Georgie,
you have some sense ; get mother to bed
and see that she swallows a beaten-up egg
with a little brandy in it—you know how
to make it—then give her the draught I
brought for her. I am going out to have
a long stroll and a smoke. I hope you
will all be gone to bed by the time I
come back."

Georgie was thankful to have some
ordinary business assigned to her, something which she could do to relax the
tension in which she too had been held,
more or less, since the day the family left
London. She bustled about obeying Pat's
orders, and carried off their mother, spent
and unresisting, to her room.

In a little time even Agnes raised her
bowed head and crept away, with her
white scared face, to her room, as if she
also gave in, however reluctantly, her act
of adherence to the fact that rest must
be sought, let the chance of its being won

be ever so small, and provision made for the dawning of a fresh day, with its fresh duties and cares.

# CHAPTER V.

In the course of a week an unforeseen incident of much moment occurred. It caused Pat, who had taken, in his uncertainty how to set about seeking for an employment, to haunt the principal chemist's shop in Quatr'eaux, to hurry home and burst into the little sitting-room above the milliner's shop with an alacrity which startled but did not alarm the occupants. The animation was not out of keeping with the manliness which had matured in a day, while it was very different from any frame of mind its owner had displayed recently. "Here's a lucky coincidence! Mother, Agnes, Georgie, I wish you all to listen. I don't know if I have happened to mention that

the principal doctor here, as I have learnt
from my friend the chemist, is a Dr.
Hubert de Vitré.   This Dr. Hubert is a
queer customer—that is, he is highly re-
spected and reckoned very skilful, but he
does not much care for his profession,
except as a means of scientific research.
He is a greater chemist than he is a doctor, and a still greater botanist and en-
tomologist.   He has a passion for hunting,
which sounds odd in a Frenchman, and
hunts twice a week in the season, in
spite of his patients, to whom nevertheless, and to the poor especially, he is
very kind and liberal, or else you may be
sure they would dismiss him for some
nincompoop of a doctor who would be
always at their beck and call.   Dr. de
Vitré is a man about forty, unmarried,
living in a big, empty-looking house, in
one of the oldest, best courtyards, near
the Cathedral.   He has a widowed sister
with her two children to keep house for

him. They say if it were not for the sister he would hardly trouble to practise, at least to send in his accounts, for he is curiously indifferent to money, and his own expenses are of the smallest."

"Well, Pat, these particulars may be interesting in so far as they have to do with the genus foreign doctor which you may be studying with fellow feeling," said Georgie, "but I fail to see how they are a lucky coincidence or in what manner they concern us."

"Wait a little—have a particle of patience," Pat recommended. "When Dr. de Vitré was pointed out to me—by the way he wore a dark green coat and a pair of long riding-boots, *outré* and unprofessional, Georgie—I had a notion that I had seen him before. It seems he also remarked me with a similar impression, and when I went to Colline's shop this morning I found this note awaiting me. Did you ever see such small fine hand-

writing—and from the fist of a mighty
hunter? Colline had told him I was
likely to settle for the present at Quatr'-
eaux and that I was looking out for employment in the medical profession. Dr.
de Vitré said he knew my face when he
saw it again. He had been in Paris and
had filled the place of one of the exam-
iners—who was called away for the day,
when I took my degree. Dr. de Vitré
was good enough to say that he was
pleased with the manner in which I had
passed my examination, and as he required an assistant, since he could not be
tied down by the drudgery of the profession, he was willing to engage my
services on trial, if I could produce
testimonials of character and if we agreed
as to terms. Evidently Colline, though
he is a friendly beggar enough, thought it
an additional proof of the doctor's eccen-
tricity that he should propose to engage
an Englishman for an assistant, granted

that I had made my studies in Paris, when he might have plenty of Frenchmen in the same capacity."

" Oh, Pat, I am so thankful for you," said his mother fervently.

" So am I for all of us," said Pat sedately.

'It is good news," pronounced Georgie excitedly. " Isn't it, Agnes ? "

" Of course," said Agnes, seeking to rid herself of the dispirited languor which was weighing her down. She was looking at the others with sad and wondering eyes. It was bad enough to have survived such a blow as they had sustained, but it was incredible that the rest of them —even her mother, whose eyes Agnes had never yet dared to meet since Mrs. Baldwin had told them all—should be prepared to enter with zest on what mattered so little as an engagement for Pat.

" He must be a nice man," speculated Georgie confidently.

"I like that," cried Pat, with the first genuine laugh which they had heard— for an age as it seemed, and the sound struck so strangely on the ears of the hearers that they looked deprecatingly first at him and then at each other. "I can tell you he is not at all a lady's man. Colline, who is a dapper, dandified wretch, like the husband of the milliner in the lower regions, says the doctor never goes into ladies' company at home, and not often into men's, unless in the pursuit of sport. He is afflicted with *mauvaise honte*, and is half a boor, half a bear. At the same time he is supposed to be very much under the thumb of madame, his widowed sister, and he makes spoiled puppets of his little nieces, her daughters."

"And is not that nice?" demanded Georgie.

"For the rest," said Pat, paying no heed to the interruption, "he is a man of science and a philosopher."

"A little awful, no doubt, to poor stupid women, but it ought to be nice to a student just off the irons, like you," insisted Georgie. "I should expect you to appreciate that."

"So I do most heartily," Pat assured her. "But look here, Georgie, you must not run off with the idea that the '*médecin malgré lui*' is going to endow me with a thumping salary—nothing of the kind. The man who is reckless in the matter of money on his own account, while he is under the thumb of an astute sister, is not likely to behave with a princely liberality to his dependants. Neither does he display much generous off-hand confidence in mankind, in making his arrangements. I am to call on him to-morrow to let him see what credentials I can furnish, and I make no question to be looked over by madame the sister, before he arrives at a decision." He stopped short suddenly, struck by the

expression in Agnes's eyes. They had
lost the faint gleam of satisfaction which
his communication had aroused in them.
The happier feeling had given place to
renewed distress. It flashed upon him
in an instant what she was thinking of,
and he acknowledged she had good reason
for her dismay. "I did not remember
that," he said quickly, in an undertone,
in answer to her look; then he added
more slowly: "Though he knew my face
I am not aware that he recalled my
name. Foreign names are always con-
fusing and puzzling to a stranger, and do
not lay hold of the ear as a native name
does—you see his note is only addressed
'To the young English doctor.'" He
walked to the window, to which Agnes
followed him. She had nothing to suggest—all she was conscious of was to
hold him back, with her feeble woman's
hands, from a gulf opening at his feet.

Georgie had not taken in the difficulty,

and if Mrs. Baldwin did so she made no sign. She did not interpose; she had forfeited her right, many a year before, to counsel her children. The brother and sister stood apart for a moment, during which Pat's mobile face grew set and stern. " I cannot publish her error and endanger her safety," he muttered in abrupt sentences; " no one could ask it of me, while there is not any reason, that I know of, why he should betray us. He looked a gentleman, if a queer one, and he bears a high character in the town. I shall tell him as much of the truth as is necessary : that we have been in family trouble and are not living under our own name, so that testimonials and certificates are no good. If he should have nothing to say to me afterwards I'm no worse off than I was before. I'd sooner risk it than begin with a tissue of lies in return for his trust in me."

" Oh, Pat, I am so glad to hear you

say so—I am so grateful to you—I am
sure it is the right course to follow," said
Agnes with her white face lighting up
for a second, just as a beam of the sun-
shine fell on her red hair converting it into
the golden crown of a queen or the nimbus
of a saint. Yet something in her words
or her look displeased him. He unloosed
the clasp of the hand which she had laid
on his arm. "You forget," he said coldly,
"that there may be danger to her in
our thus appeasing our consciences and
being consoled—so far at her expense.
We are bound not to lose sight of her in
whatever we say or do. I cannot believe
there is much danger, else I would bite
my tongue out before I said anything.
But if this Dr. de Vitré should turn out
an inquisitive gossip he might ferret
out more than I choose to tell of the tale
which she has thought fit to conceal all
these years. Mind, I still think it well
for her and all to make the admission I

am prepared to make. But it strikes me, Agnes, you lose sight of her and forget what is owing to her, when all is said and done."

She fell back at his rebuke. Was it true that she lost sight of her mother, that she forgot what was due to her motherhood in condemning her lamentable lapse from truth and womanliness? If so she could not help it, her whole nature was in revolt—but what a miserable girl she was to be harsh and pitiless to her own mother.

"It is only right and natural that madame as well as monsieur the doctor should see you before he engages you," Georgie told him when he turned back from his consultation with Agnes in the window. "I should have no objection for madame to look me over also if that would be any use."

"Not the slightest," asserted Pat a little sarcastically; "she would simply be tempted to regard you as a forward, strong-minded English girl."

Pat reported himself at Dr. de Vitré's house, but of what passed privately between him and the doctor Pat did not speak even to Agnes. She could only judge of the result from the fact that the engagement was concluded, and her brother was in fairly good spirits and more like himself again. He was quite ready to talk of what he called "the barracks of a house" in the quaint court, with trees in the background, a flower border and a draw well. The floors of the rooms were painfully polished and dangerously slippery, but the staircase—he wished Georgie could see the stairs. He was sure she could not resist flying at them with a mop and a broom and oceans of soap and water He had to admit that Dr. de Vitré had behaved like a gentleman, albeit an odd gentleman, in the transaction. Moreover, Madame

Paradol his sister had been quite civil. She was the perfection of *bourgeois* good breeding and good preservation. She had been positively gracious when she had told him that he might have the pleasure of spending each Sunday with his excellent family. Of course that was to save his board, for he had to board with his boss, and not to have him tacked on to the de Vitré-Paradol Sunday receptions, excursions into the forest, drives in the country, and—and—well, "Barkis was willin'." He did not mind a bit being cut off from the de Vitré-Paradol festivities, neither would Georgie howl, he daresayed, at having him to keep her in order one day in seven.

Howl! it was the single compensation to Georgie for a separation she might have foreseen. Agnes was dull company nowadays, and poor mother was what Georgie had always known her. Nay, she was even a more dead-alive figure

than she had looked before the floodgates
were burst open, and she had disbur-
dened herself of her sorry secret. For her
restless fingers were at rest ; there was no
further call for the incessant motion
which had formed at once a safety valve
and a veil for the troubled spirit, behind
the working hands and clicking needles.
It appeared as if Quatr'eaux would have
been a stony desert to Georgie, without a
weekly glimpse of Pat and an opportunity
to chatter to him. But she was soon to
have another resource. When she was out
on her marketing expeditions she was
fond of just taking a look at Pat's quar-
ters. She would slacken her steps and
watch surreptitiously for the chance opening of the great gates and the revelation
of the cool spacious court with its gum-
cistus bushes, sunflowers and tubs with
aloes, which she was sure Madame Paradol cherished as a mark of gentility, and
its dog couch for the doctor's huge mastiff

"Lion," which Pat said was to keep away tramps like Georgie. Lion did not cause any alarm to two little girls in white frocks whom Georgie sometimes saw flitting about the court, like a pair of white pigeons.

In the confinement and stifling atmosphere of the little *étage* above the milliner's shop, which was far worse than the small house at Barnes, the girl took to contemplating the doctor's big house, in its shady court, with pensive longing as an earthly paradise. To serve for an excuse to pass the place daily, no less than to attempt something on her own account, Georgie collected all the drawing and painting materials among her luggage, and boldly attacked the Cathedral. She intrepidly sketched and worked up little views upon views of the sculptured front, the grey towers round which the ivy clung and the rooks circled, the rose window, the cleristory, the baptistery, the chapter house,

the pilgrims' tombs. What she was inclined to consider as still more dauntless
on her part, she walked into a print shop
and offered, in her stammering French, her
daubs for sale. To her agreeable surprise
the proprietor of the shop condescended
to look at them and let them remain in
his window ; to her abiding, unbounded
astonishment he sold some of them, enough
to encourage Georgie, as she had never
been encouraged before, to work seriously
and steadily—"not that I shall ever make
anything of art, unless, perhaps, a little
money which I shall by no means under-
value, for which I shall be devoutly
thankful." She gave a passing sigh and
then continued to speak with admirable
equanimity : "I have not the soul of
a painter, as you have the soul of a story-
teller, Agnes."

"Nonsense, Georgie," said Agnes tartly ;
"you know I always told you that you
would paint some day if you had patience."

Agnes could not be indifferent to the success which she had so long predicted and prayed for, Georgie's success, for which she would well-nigh have sacrificed her own, at any time, which might make up for her, Agnes's, defeat. Her sun might have set, her spirit be broken, but it would be something to have Pat and Georgie fulfil her expectations. It was intolerable to have Georgie continue to talk mock-modest affected nonsense about not being a painter.

"I know best," said Georgie with decision, shaking her comely head philosophically over the washing of her brushes : "I tell you I am not the real article, but I know it when I see it. This very morning I met two *rauriens*, with long hair, and red caps perched on the sides of their heads. The men smelt of tobacco-smoke and absinthe, as they came behind me, and put the Cathedral towers into their sketch-books in fewer minutes than

I should have taken to arrange my paper
or canvas, use my rule, and start with my
first straight line. I got a glimpse of
their work as I turned, and there was
the true Cathedral of which I was making
a gingerly china-plate, Christmas-card
version. I do not mean to praise the
artists in other respects. They were
horrid fellows. I am not sure that they
were quite sober. I should have been
rather frightened to be in their company
if there had not been plenty of people
about. One of the two was rude enough
to poke his head under my hat to examine
my poor affair. But I saw what the man
was after, packed up my wares and walked
away majestically, I flatter myself. Oh,
yes, you need not be frightened—I can
take care of myself when I go about alone,
every whit as well as if I had twenty
chaperons. I can do it, though Frenchmen
are not accustomed to any girl above the
rank of a milliner's apprentice going about

alone, and they have the poorest opinion of girls who are artists. Still Frenchmen will not be impertinent to English girls who can be *farouches* when liberties are taken with them. All the same these unpleasant compatriots of Corot and Millet were painters, Agnes, though they were not nature's gentlemen, and their work was art, even I could see that. Why the shop in the Place can take my bits and leave theirs, if the sketches were offered to the shopman, I cannot imagine."

"You are not fair to yourself," said Agnes, jealous for her sister.

But Georgie was perfectly fair, and she was clear-sighted and correct in the conclusion at which she arrived : "What I find is making a sale for copies of pretty bits of the Cathedral just now, is that the present bishop's jubilee is about to be celebrated. He is a popular old man, and instead of attempting to murder him as the inhabitants of Quatr'eaux did to the mediæval bishop whose statue is in the market-place, their descendants are busy buying little pictures of the present bishop's Cathedral as memorials of his rule. Naturally the great proportion of the flock prefer prettiness and pettiness to something rough, sombre and grand. I have come at a lucky time for me, and for all of us, and I must make hay while the sun shines."

Georgie might be matter-of-fact and mercenary, but she shook off her idleness and was also diligent and in earnest in what she saw bear fruit. The out-of-door occupation superseded for the moment the household cares, and was at least a fine promoter of the worker's health of body and peace of mind. To Agnes's horror she heard Georgie say carelessly, one day, that she had never been so busy and so happy in her life. Then Pat who was present chimed in, with his keen enjoyment of Dr. de Vitré's laboratory. Oh, what could they be thinking of? It was like the nearest relatives and dearest friends of the newly dead finding life fuller than before, as bright and hopeful as ever, without these vanished personalities with which their fellows had once been so familiar, in all the sweet influences and cheerful homely incidents of every-day life. Agnes could not have said why Pat and Georgie in their youth, should not be speedily reconciled to their mother and the world, only it was impossible for her. She was scandalized while a humble, trembling gratitude, most piteous to behold, stole into the sunken eyes of the dead-alive figure in their midst—because two of her children were comforted and content.

# CHAPTER VI.

THE domestic duties which had been formerly discharged by Georgie devolved on
Agnes, until it seemed as if she and her
sister had changed places. Agnes strove
not to fail, and in ordinary circumstances
her genius would have vindicated itself
here as elsewhere. But its wings were
drooping and draggled, though the stains
they had contracted were not from any
act of hers. Foreign ways of doing confused and bewildered her, when she had
no longer the high spirit to master them
at a bound, and to enjoy the mastery as
she had enjoyed every other contest with
difficulties.

Worst of all, though she never forgot
her mother's requirements and was fain

to minister to them, Agnes still shrank
from her mother unconquerably, in a
manner that was exquisitely painful for
the shrinker and the person shrunk from
to realize, and distressing even for the
initiated bystander to witness.

"Agnes, how can you be so hard on
poor mother?" Georgie did not hesitate
to reproach her sister when the two were
alone together in what Georgie called
their cupboard of a bedroom. "I do not
mean that you do not attend to her wants,
and try to make her comfortable in a
strange place—of course you do. But it
is a hard task for you, and you cannot
hide that it is so. You are no better
company for her than she is for you, yet
I used to think you adored mother; I was
half jealous of the way in which she would
brighten up when you came in, or if there
was any question of you in our plans.
I wonder at you. If she erred she has
repented—repented bitterly, and she was

thinking of us and our interests all the time."

"Georgie, what kind of thinking was it that could cause her to commit a heart- less fraud merely that we might not be poor?" cried Agnes with intense bitter- ness. "It is so terrible to think that she should never have loved father and yet have married him, like cold-blooded women of the world whom one reads of. And when she saw him lying dead at her feet, where almost any other woman with a woman's heart in her breast would have been overwhelmed with horror and pity for his sad fate, she was sufficiently mistress of herself to agree to be one in a sordid cheat, to save herself and us from the consequences of his rash act. You don't remember father, I do. The last time he rode out he made me go with him on my pony, and on my last birthday in his lifetime he filled my little book-case with the books I chose.

Now I have lost mother as well as father. I know that you and Pat think I am hard and unforgiving, and that such a character will gradually repel you till you cease to care for me—I know that she believes that I do not love her any longer. How can I when I am father's daughter as well as mother's? But it is horrible to feel it coming true."

Agnes's face was all quivering with emotion; Georgie was a little paler than usual, but she was calm. She advanced and patted Agnes in mingled remonstrance and reassurance on the shoulder. " Don't, Agnes, don't; where is the good of torturing yourself and everybody else? The thing is long past and done with, in the deed if not in its effects. We may be thankful that the insurance company failed when it did, though no doubt it ruined many poor people at the time. You are wincing, but only think what it would have been if we had got arrears of money to pay back, without the means of paying it? We must have done it somehow; it had got to be paid if we had taken it without any right to it and spent it. But we might have slaved, and slaved, and grown grey-headed before the debt was discharged. I am sure you are the last girl to quarrel with bearing such consequences as have fallen on us, for the sake of those we are bound to love and honour. Mother was wrong, and she is sorry; father too must have been wrong —you must be fair to mother and see that—but it is all long past and over. What we have to do is to forget and forgive, and make the best of our share of the penalty."

It was all very true, but it was easy for Georgie to speak. Her faith had not been rudely shaken, her dreams dispelled. She had not been wrapped up in a fond belief in the intrinsic worth of those who had gone before her, nay, of humanity itself. She had not idealized and idolized a mourning mother.

Pat, in his capacity of medical man, did not like the extent to which Agnes lost flesh and the continuance of her depression. He suspected there was danger of her getting more and more absorbed in her special grievance, and drifting farther and farther from general interests. She was not her mother's daughter for nothing. He came one Sunday evening to lend himself to a proposal of Madame Paradol's, which he thought might be good for his sister.

Madame had asked him, after the most polite fashion, whether his sister, who drew and painted and consented to dispose of her work, might not be induced to give madame's little girls lessons daily, in English and music more particularly. Madame had heard of the thoroughness of an English education, so she had no

doubt that the young lady who painted to
a marvel also knew how to play and
sing, while it went without saying that
she must be well acquainted with her
mother tongue.    Madame would be
charmed to have the benefit of an
English instructress for her daughters,
and she ventured to trust the benefit
might be mutual.    She would do everything in her power to make the young
lady happy and to render her stay in
a foreign town, where she knew nobody out of the circle of her estimable
family, less *triste* than it must otherwise be.

"In short," Pat announced to the
estimable family, "madame is so greedy
of any advantage for those mites of hers
that she is willing to include their
governess in those Paradol-de-Vitré
gaieties from which I, wretched mortal,
have been hitherto banished."

"But how can I go to madame's,

Pat," objected Georgie, "when I have all these commissions on my hands?"

In spite of the objection it was clear that she had no disinclination to accept the overture. In fact her eyes sparkled at the mention of it. "I can see the commissions are not likely to last, and the engagement to teach madame's children may be more permanent; still I should not like to lose all these francs which I have been promised, in addition to breaking my promise to earn them. Would not Agnes do in my place in the meantime? She says she cannot write since she came abroad; don't you say so, Agnes?" appealing to her sister, who had hardly roused herself from the silent sorrowful abstraction becoming habitual to her. "You have not even attempted to put down the verses of a song to set to music, such as you used to knock off—in Pat's phrase—in a couple of hours; you have not so much as opened the piano

which I took it upon me to hire, to try
if it would inspire you. A spell of
teaching might be good for you."

"So I think, most wise Georgie," com-
mented Pat, "accordingly I took it upon
me to hint to madame that if Miss
Georgie Raimes was a clever and accomplished young woman, Miss Agnes, or
Miss Raimes, I beg her pardon, was even
cleverer and more accomplished."

"I'll go if you wish it," said Agnes,
but her tone was utterly indifferent and
her feet dragged wearily, as she quitted
the room.

Mrs. Baldwin looked up quickly with
a rare flash of indignation in her eyes.
"Why set Agnes to a task which is so
unworthy of her?" she asked sharply.

"Because she needs the task," said
Pat quietly, and his mother said no more,
though it was plain she groaned in
spirit.

"Between you and me, Geo," Pat

told his younger sister the next time
they were alone together, " if Agnes is
not roused she will go the way of the
poor mater. I never saw such a change
on a girl in my life ; but that is neither
here nor there. Madame was very
gracious—she is always gracious, even
when she is making poor shy, gruff de
Vitré do the honours of her *salon*, the
reverse of what he wishes to do. Either
of my sisters, she said, would only be
too charming, too perfect as a teacher
for Félicité and Nicolaise. I can promise
Agnes that, barring a little patronage,
madame will prove an agreeable employer.
As for the mites, they are not ducks
but pigeons. Did you ever watch
pigeons going mincing and bridling on
their pink feet, shaking their little white
heads, with their air of incomparable art-
lessness and propriety ? That is just
like Félice and Nicole. They are
drowned, swallowed up in mannerliness

and decorum, but behind it all they are nice little pigeons in their way."

" Then Agnes shall have the charge of them and possess the *entrée* to madame's *salon*, for I suppose that is what she means, if it will do poor dear Agnes any good," said Georgie magnanimously. "To think that we should welcome such a change —any change for her," added the speaker with a suspicion of moisture dimming her straightforward sensible eyes, but twinkled away the next minute. "That Agnes's energies should want to be stirred up when we could never keep pace with her in the old days! I should have liked well enough to go and impart English and what not to the Mesdemoiselles Paradol. I should have liked to make the acquaintance, in the most modest manner, of the learned Doctor and his well-bred sister, and your pigeons, and of those of the good folks of Quatr'eaux who are admitted as *habitués* of the house;

I confess to a pining to walk round that delectable court and look at the flowers, since I no longer have flowers of my own, not even in a snip of a town garden. I am not proud and I could have kept my place, taking amusement out of everything and everybody, I hope without being spiteful. I don't tire of my own company—our own company, but a little variety for a change is not to be despised, is it? However, it is certain I do not need a change so much as Agnes needs it, and if it is any good to Agnes, why, there is no more to be said."

Agnes made no demur, and doubtless the mere fact of being several hours of each day in another person's house, and of having a regular occupation again was of some use to her, though there was little improvement to be detected in her spirits. She went punctually to Dr. de Vitré's house and taught his nieces, "giving satisfaction" to the authorities. But the atmosphere of enthusiasm which had formerly surrounded her and lent her such an attraction was dispersed, fled as if for ever. She felt no enthusiasm for her work or for her pupils. They entertained no enthusiasm for her, though they liked her, in a half frightened, half wondering way, a good deal better than their last instructress. *She* was capricious and peevish, while it did not make up for her inconstant humours that when she escaped the vigilant eyes of madame, the lady was inclined to confide to her small audience her squabbles with her landladies and her affairs with her lovers.

Madame wrinkled up her pronounced nose when she contemplated "Mees Raines." She was such a thorough English girl; she was so absent-minded that she would start and colour when her name was spoken; she was always grave in her gentleness. Though she taught music she never played or sang on her own ac-

22—2

count, indeed her voice had sustained the strange transformation which grief works in some voices. Its clear ringing notes were grown hoarse and husky. Still, these Englishwomen have consciences, and this one had her value as a teacher. Another thing to be noted, Agnes without her enthusiasm, her radiant faith in God and man, was but a dull, white-faced, red-haired girl, singularly without charm in Madame Paradol's estimation, and therefore, as madame congratulated herself, a perfectly safe person to be introduced into the household the head of which was an eccentric bachelor.

Then it fell on a week-day when Pat was not expected in the little side street in which the family lodged, that he walked in, mounting the stair two steps at a time, though the weather was very hot. He had a light in his eye and a colour in his cheek which indicated that he brought news for them ; something out

of what was rapidly becoming their common round of duties and obligations had
happened.

"What is it?" inquired Georgie, looking up from the bit of pillow-lace she
was learning to weave. She was rarely
so much taken aback or impressed as to
refrain from asking an explanation of
what had come to pass.

On the contrary Mrs. Baldwin and
Agnes, who had come in a little before
Pat, sat staring in silence with a scared
look on their faces, which brought out
the latent likeness between them start-
lingly for an instant.

"Mother," said Pat, standing before
Mrs. Baldwin, "there was one topic which
I thought never to revive between us, no,
nor in anybody else's hearing. But I
must speak of it this once before you
all. I have heard again from Scrope.
You, I, all of us are free to return to
England when we will. The wretched

fellow whom you called Tweedside John-nie is dead. He was in the care of the police till his half-raving story could be seen to. He was found dead in a police cell. As he would have been the principal witness in the accusation which he made, and as nobody has pressed the charge after all these years, the matter has been suffered to drop. Nothing farther will be done; there will be no criminal investigation."

"And no public exposure," said Mrs. Baldwin with a long sigh of relief. "My boy, I am thankful for your and your sisters' sakes. God has been better to me than I deserved."

"I suppose it is a blessing," said Georgie doubtfully, "though we were here under another name and were not likely to be found out. Besides, if any part of the truth is known, I always think it is better the whole should come to light, until scandal can make nothing worse of it, and there is no more to be apprehended."

Nobody seconded her. As for Agnes she was thinking of things of which there could be no undoing, no restitution. Could the silence of law and justice for evermore give her back the tender, admiring thoughts of her mother which she had cherished six months ago ?

" The question is," said Pat rapidly, almost blusteringly, as if he were in haste to finish the discussion, " are we to return to England with the next train and steamer ? Are we to forego all the advantages we have painfully scraped together in our expatriation ? "

" It must be as you and the girls will, Pat," said Mrs. Baldwin. " It is sufficient for me to be with my children— that they do not cast me off."

" No, indeed," said Georgie emphatically, " and I for one don't wish to go back to England. A bird in the hand is worth two in the bush. We can live more cheaply here, till we make our fortunes. I never got a commission in England—I don't suppose I ever should."

"And I feel as I never thought to feel, half a Frenchman by this time," said Pat eagerly, and in point of fact he gave his shoulders a true French shrug—a shrug he had not acquired during all the time of study in Paris. "I have no assistant practice to go back to at Barnes. De Vitré is showing me a thing or two here. I like the life, the man. What do you say, Agnes? Will it spoil your prospects as a writer to remain abroad?"

"Oh, no, no!" cried Agnes. "I have no prospects—I am no writer—I don't wish to go back to England," and she gave a scarcely perceptible shudder, as the idea of having to face Sam Scrope, of being so much nearer to Brackengill, was forced upon her.

So England sank down beneath the Baldwins' horizon, and all they heard of it was in an occasional friendly letter from

Sam Scrope to Pat. Once or twice Sam inclosed a letter from one or other of his good-natured sisters to Georgie, but they were letters difficult to answer, because they were evidently written in a state of bewilderment, on the writer's part, as to what had taken the Baldwins to Normandy and what was keeping them there.

But though Pat did not return to England he was shrewd enough and courageous enough to take a step, which should render his staying away, thenceforth, entirely a matter of choice and not of compulsion. He promptly resumed the latter half of his name, candidly telling all whom the change could concern that he had merely dropped the Baldwin half, for a purpose and a season. He was Baldwin, and of course his mother and sisters were Baldwins likewise—an assertion which they ratified, Mrs. Baldwin with her new sense of thankfulness, Georgie joyfully shaking herself, as if to get rid of false impressions and re-establish her identity, even Agnes brightening a little as she glanced at her signet ring. The Baldwins had not been long enough in Quatr'eaux for the change of their name to create a deep and widely-spread sensation. For that matter some of the inhabitants—including the man-milliner and his wife—cheerfully adapted themselves to the situation, and looked and spoke as if it was the natural and usual arrangement for English residents to try living in France under *aliases*.

Madame was the most disturbed by the transformation ; it shook her faith in the rampant respectability of " these English," though it did not cause her to have no farther need for Agnes's services as gover-ness to madame's daughters. But as for Dr. de Vitré, he received and adopted the correction in the address of his assistant with the greatest serenity. Certainly the man of science was neither inquisitive nor a gossip.

# CHAPTER VII.

## "LET ME DIE FOR MY LITTLE AGNES."

THE summer, which had sometimes appeared incredibly long, sometimes marvellously short to the Baldwins, just as they viewed it according to the number and extent of the changes it had introduced into the family life, or according to the hurry and bustle attendant on these changes, was passing into autumn. Nothing of greater importance had taken place quite recently than that Georgie had received an additional commission or two for choice bits of the Cathedral; Pat had been introduced by Dr. de Vitré—a mark of attention which "little Baldwin" had the grace and perception to regard as a high compliment—to some congenial spirits where the doctor was concerned, one or two *savants* and naturalists, as devoted and single-hearted as himself, established in the neighbourhood; Agnes had appeared occasionally in madame's *salon*, or gone with her and the children on their excursions into the forest, or to the country houses in the vicinity, without deriving a tithe of the pleasure—she who had once been so receptive of impressions —which Georgie would have experienced in similar circumstances. Mrs. Baldwin was out of count as she had been for many a day—nay, with the second crisis of her life past, with nothing more to fear, as there was nothing more to hope, the grey of the coming night was fast descending on her.

Mrs. Baldwin and her daughter were together in their little *salon*, Mrs. Baldwin quiescent in her chair, her thin blanched hands resting passively in the lap of her black gown, her dim eyes looking up into the unfathomable twilight sky.

Georgie, who had set up a miniature *jardinière*, was employing a few spare moments in snipping off dead leaves and blossoms, poking up the earth between, watering from her tiny watering-pan and generally tidying and refreshing her liliputian parterre.

Agnes was correcting a handful of exercises in half-text, the fruit of the Demoiselles Paradol's labours. In order to help her in her task in the twilight, she had lit the lamp on a little round table by her side, and the light was falling not on the exercises alone but also on her tall slight figure and bent head. She was not dressed according to her inclinations, which might have pointed to heavy black, if not to sackcloth and ashes. She wore a white muslin frock in honour of a half-holiday and a *réunion* at madame's, from which Agnes had just been liberated.

One moment all was apparently cheerful content or despairing resignation, peace and industry in the little room, the next all was wild confusion and terror.

By an involuntary movement Agnes knocked over the rickety table and dashed the lamp to the ground. There was the clash of the fall, half lost in the stunning report of an explosive spirit, and the dazzling flash and strong fumes of a pyramid of flame, where Agnes had been thrown down by the shock.

Georgie started round to fly to her sister's aid, snatching up the woollen table-cover and calling for help as she did so. But before she could reach Agnes, Mrs. Baldwin was by her daughter, dragging her aside, folding her close in the mother's arms, wrapping the mother's dress round her to extinguish the fire which was catching the girl's clothes. In another instant the man-milliner and his partner in his business and his affections rushed upon the scene, summoned by Georgie's screams, and by means of poker and shovel and wet blankets beat and stamped and stifled the enemy, till nothing was left of his crest of flame save a tall column of dense white smoke which continued for some time to rise mysteriously from the floor, out of which an Arabian geni might have been expected to step at any moment. Mademoiselle was saved, the house and business were saved, the man-milliner continued to cry triumphantly. Georgie stopped him and begged him to fetch her brother or Dr. de Vitré if Dr. Baldwin was not at hand, without loss of time.

Agnes was absolutely unscorched, though the skirt of her dress was singed and shrivelled up, yet she lay insensible with a face like marble, and half open, unseeing eyes.

Mrs. Baldwin's woollen gown was positively charred and her hands and wrists were badly burned, as Georgie could see to her dismay, but her mother uttered no complaint and gave no sign of pain; there was even the faintest smile of self-devotion hovering about her parted lips,

while she kept muttering, " Let me die
for her, yes, let me die for my little
Agnes," as she hung over her daughter.

Pat came immediately, accompanied by
Dr. de Vitré, because of the imperative,
alarming nature of the summons.  Neither
of the men made light of the accident, or
said there was no call for the presence
of both of them.  Pat was as serious as
a judge, though he overcame his natural
distress.  Dr. de Vitré lost his shyness
and discomfiture at intruding on com-
parative strangers.  He was all alertness
and interest as when he was carried along
in the spirit of the chase, or absorbed in
the solution of some scientific puzzle.
" Did you ever see your sister like this
before, Baldwin ? " he inquired briskly.

" Never," answered Pat briefly.

" Has she suffered from any illness, or sustained any shock previous to this accident,
which might intensify its effects ? "  To
hear him one would not have supposed that

he had been in the habit of seeing Agnes almost every day for a period of weeks. But his nieces' governess, even his assistant's sister, was somebody very different from an interesting patient.

"No illness, but I have feared the gradual continuous lowering of her system after a family trial which she had to face," said Pat with an effort.

"Oh!" exclaimed the older man, remembering something, while a flash of his black eyes took in Mrs. Baldwin's bowed, arrested figure. "But that, though it is to be regretted in itself, like any other misadventure, is rather a hopeful element in the present case, it may account for the extreme prostration, even for the prolonged insensibility. She must be got to bed, kept in a proper temperature and stimulated and nourished by every possible means. I think she is beginning to come to herself," letting his hand fall from Agnes's fluttering pulse. "Now, madam," with a strong hand raising Mrs. Baldwin, giving her his arm and seating her in her accustomed chair, "let me see to your burns." It was the greatest comfort and support to Georgie, in the emergency, to have two men possessed of knowledge and skill to say what was to be done ; and to order her about while she ran here and there doing their bidding and following up their hints with admirable directness and intelligence. She had only once before obeyed Pat, without stopping to talk the matter over and dispute his inferences, but now she deferred to him implicitly and treated him, not to say Dr. de Vitré, as if he were a Solon. It was about Agnes clearly that the doctors were most concerned, and it was to her that they devoted their chief attention. Indeed, Mrs. Baldwin would hardly allow them to do otherwise ; she suffered her burns to be dressed with scarcely subdued impatience, and did not

take time to express any relief she felt,
so intent was she on transferring all the
care to Agnes. "Go to your sister, Pat.
Dr. de Vitré, it is my daughter who needs
you," was her constant cry. For even
after Agnes had partially recovered, her
breath came in such little trembling
gasps, her pulse was so weak and fluttering, she had such a far-away look in her
blue-grey eyes, her consciousness continued so obscured, that it seemed for
many hours as if she were still hovering
on the border-land between life and
death; as if the least untoward touch
would precipitate her over the brink, and
the greatest efforts and precautions were
wanted to fan the life which had ebbed
so low.

It was only after Agnes was a great
deal better, and Pat had confidently assured everybody that she had turned the
corner and would be all right again in no
time, that Georgie took him aside and

communicated to him her uneasiness regarding their mother. "I don't think mother can be going on quite rightly, Pat ; I have almost to force her to swallow food. I have been feeding her because of her poor hands, but between us we make a poor job of it."

"I daresay," returned Pat in a matter-of-course tone ; "she cannot be expected to display much of an appetite when she is in such pain, though she bears it very patiently ; but of course we must not let her strength go down."

"Pat," interposed Georgie anxiously, "I don't believe she has pain, I don't really. I am not sure that she feels anything. And have you noticed that she has always referred to Agnes, since her accident, as if she were not grown-up, as if she were a child again ?"

Pat looked startled, but he was unwilling to acknowledge any ground for fresh alarm. "Nonsense, Georgie, you women are always imagining things, though I did think that *you* were more reasonable—that it was facts, not fancies, with you. Why, de Vitré was quite complimentary about you. He said he had never, till he came across you, seen a woman, short of a professional nurse, who could act instead of speaking, and had not to wait to make apologies, indulge in digressions and extract praise, before she obeyed orders and attended to her patients. He was struck with a girl like you being so ready and handy. He asked if the run of English girls were as clear-headed and useful."

"I am much obliged to Dr. de Vitré," said Georgie with a passing demureness; "I hope you said I was a favourable specimen. But it is mother, not myself, I wish to speak about."

"Another marvel in a young woman," declared Pat. "But how can you tell what mother feels when she says so little about her feelings? As to speaking of

Agnes as 'little Agnes,' that may be easily accounted for—I daresay the accident recalled some incident of her childhood. Mother may even wander a little without anything far amiss, considering her age— she is old for her years—all she has gone through, the shock of this beastly lamp business and the pain she is suffering. Don't you get nervous, Georgie, after you have behaved beautifully and won laurels."

" She is not suffering," repeated Georgie gravely, and he did not contradict her or pooh-pooh her fears when his attention was drawn to his mother lying placidly on her bed, moving her bound-up hands as if they were free and uninjured, look- ing at him with shining eyes and asking when little Agnes would be about again, she was such an active child she could never bear to be still. Besides she, her mother, depended upon the child—now nurse was gone and the establishment so

much reduced—to look after the little
ones.

It was on Mrs. Baldwin's case that the
two doctors' energies were bent after all,
and bent in vain. She grew worse instead of better, and so rapidly that
her medical attendants recognized her
constitution had been breaking up beforehand, and that her condition, whether
overlooked as it had been, or perceived
from the first, would have been to a
great extent hopeless. She was in no
pain and she was happy, for the first
time for many a year, Pat could assure
poor Georgie ; in fact the sick woman's
own words often murmured were all to
the same effect : " I am so glad to be let
die for little Agnes. Yes, God has
been far better to me than I deserved.
Agnes is so young and gifted, she will
grow up not only a good but a great
woman ; she will do a thousand times
more for Pat and Baby than I could ever

have done; she will bring no shame on them; she will never be weak and wicked whatever temptation may assail her. She will be a blessing to her generation when she is grown a woman—my bright, unfearing, untiring little Agnes."

Mrs. Baldwin's peace was only disturbed when Agnes was permitted to rise from her sick-bed and go to her mother before it was too late.

"Mother, mother," cried Agnes piteously, as her mother failed to greet her, simply turning to her wondering, questioning eyes, in which the light was fast fading. "Do you not know me, and you have been so hurt coming to my help? None but you, mother, could have done it; I might have been burnt to death but for you, though Georgie would have done her best; still none but you would have forgotten everything for me, and I—I have caused you so much pain."

"Agnes!" cried her mother doubtfully.

" Why, how big you have grown, and you
are not like yourself.  It is not only that
you are thin, you look so sad, and you
are hardly ever sad, and never, never
dull."  Then as if a gleam of intelligence
recalled all to her for a momentary space,
" I have been dreaming," she said, " but I
am awake now."  She smiled again and repeated with a difference : " Let me die for
my big Agnes, my grown-up girl, my
eldest daughter, who is so good and so
clever, the stay and bread-winner of the
family."

" No, no, mother, it is all changed,"
said Agnes sorrowfully.  " It is Pat and
Georgie who are doing almost everything
now.  Perhaps it is right they should
have their turn, but I have been so stupid,
so foolish, yet I never meant to be
cruel."

" Not cruel, my dear," corrected her
mother quickly ; " you were too high-
minded, too pure and brave either to sus-

pect evil or to understand the weight of temptation."

"Say rather, I was too wilful and un-yielding, too intolerant and self-righteous. Mother, you must live for my sake, to see how I'll learn to understand and sym-pathize," urged Agnes.

"Hush! child," said her mother softly, "life and death are not in my keeping any more than in yours; but I can see that I am going to die for your sake, and that it is far better than that I should live. Your tender, loving heart will be caught in the rebound; you will magnify the little service I have been permitted to do for you; and oh! Agnes, I have been pardoned and blessed in doing it. I have felt that—far above any pain—I, your un-worthy mother, have been allowed to save you, and you will remember that and for-get all else; my shortcomings will be lost sight of, my sin cancelled. Little Agnes, what have I been saying? Surely it is getting dark ; it is time you were in bed—it is time that all of us were asleep."

Mrs. Baldwin was right in that glimpse of knowledge which came to her. She saw more clearly than Agnes saw, in that light, which is neither piercingly clear nor bewilderingly dark, that prevails where the world of sense and the world of spirit meet. Death, and only such a death, could give back to Agnes the mother of her youth. " Sing something to me, Agnes," said Mrs. Baldwin wistfully, rousing herself once, and only once again, from the billows and depths of unconsciousness which were closing over her. Agnes hesitated, and had nearly broken down. Then with a great effort she sang, and her voice sounded through the little room with something of its old penetrating sweetness :

> "Faint and weary, lone and dreary,
>    Through the desert Thou did'st go."

In the company of One who carried our

griefs and bore our sorrows, and was bruised for our iniquities, the traveller departed on her far journey.

When all was over, though the very flood-gates of Agnes's nature were opened and she wept till she could weep no more, she was at peace. The thought of her mother who had died to rescue her effaced the memory of that other woman who had looked down on the drowned body of her husband, and calculated how the conceal-ment of the nature of his death might secure to her and her children ease and comfort, instead of the abject poverty she shrank from. The ugly phantom which had pursued Agnes, the horror and re-pugnancy which had haunted and crushed her, were gone never to return. Her mother's errors were indeed blotted out so far as Agnes Baldwin was concerned. The spot where Mrs. Baldwin was laid, in French earth, would be dear and sacred to Agnes, even more than to her sister

and brother, as long as life lasted—so
dear, that standing among its willows and
cypresses she could bear to think of that
other grave in England, among the mossy
grey stones of a north country churchyard
near Brackengill, in which her father's
dust rested. She could trust that somehow, sometime, all the mistakes and mis-
understandings between the pair, the omis-
sions still more than the commissions,
the wrong-doing in which they took part,
would pass away, condoned by the Great
Wrong - Sufferer and Wrong - Vanquisher,
until the couple knew and loved each
other as they had not known and loved
each other on earth.

And when time, the healer, had done
his work, Agnes's voice broke forth again,
clear and full, with a pathos which it
had not held before, in "psalms and
hymns and spiritual songs." Her pen
ran rapidly over the paper once more,
working for bread, but still eager as ever

to express her conceptions of the true and the beautiful—which are one and the same. Above all things she strove with unutterable striving, which had in its very elements a mixture of high delight and humble anguish, because her words faltered and failed, to express how in God's glorious providence He can bring light out of darkness and good out of evil:

> " Out of the snow the snowdrop,
> Out of death—life."

# CHAPTER VIII.

In the first Easter vacation after the Baldwins' establishment in Quatr'eaux and Mrs. Baldwin's death, Agnes happened to be alone in the sitting-room over the milliner's shop. It was not Sunday and Pat was of course absent, so was Georgie. Her little spark of achievement and success as an artist had died out as quickly as it had sprung up. Fortunately she had suspected its ephemeral nature from the beginning. The *furore* for her pretty wishy-washy little sketches had passed away with the old bishop's jubilee. When Agnes resumed her literary work, Georgie willingly took her sister's place as instructress of the small Paradol maidens. The exchange was not altogether to madame's mind, though the damsels welcomed it. But their mother refrained from demurring, an act of self-restraint for which she would never cease to reproach herself. The truth was, she feared, to begin with, that she would lose altogether the unusual advantage in Quatr'eaux of being able to secure, at a very moderate salary, the services of a well-trained English day governess for her daughters. A little later, to demur would simply have been to precipitate an appalling catastrophe, which as yet only lurked in the background, and madame was far too politic to ruin herself in this silly, rash way.

Dr. de Vitré had from the first approved of Georgie as Agnes's successor. Indeed, he had shown more interest in the change than he was in the habit of testifying with regard to his sister's domestic arrangements. He had been particularly struck by Georgie's sound sense, her practicality and helpfulness in the room of swoons and sobs and ill-timed lamentations on the night of the accident to her sister and mother. He took to Georgie as he had taken to Pat, at the first glance. He was pleased with her method of teaching his nieces, and when he had overcome his shyness in addressing her he found her a wonderfully clear-headed available auxiliary, during her brother's inevitable absence, in the doctor's innumerable scientific experiments. Madame, the experimenter's sister, was of little use in this respect, and detested the job, while Félice and Nicole were too young to act as her substitutes. It was decidedly against madame's judgment that her daughters' instructress should also be her brother's assistant. However, the servants bungled, and now and then the outwardly gruff but inwardly mild *savant* stood at bay and defied his tyrant's authority, especially on any question which had to do with his beloved science.

As Agnes sat alone in the *salon*, a big man in an overcoat, looking like a huge phlegmatic giant to the airy, lively man-milliner and his wife, walked unceremoniously into the shop of fashionable fabrics, and inquired in his slow, thick English tongue for the family of his compatriots who occupied the *étage* above the shop. Receiving permission, he mounted the rickety stair with a strong, firm step which threatened to shake it to its foundation, and was ushered into "Mees Baldwin's" presence, by the perturbed *concierge* and proprietor in one. The latter was trembling for the safety of his property under the tread and handling of a genuine John Bull, not an agreeable *petit-maître* like the young doctor, who represented the male element in the Baldwin household.

Agnes looked up from some needlework with which she was engaged, saw Sam Scrope standing before her and re-

membered how she had last parted from
him after their encounter in the park.
A gush of tears sprang to her eyes
as she rose from her seat, and her head
seemed to spin round, so that she had
to grasp the back of her chair for
an instant to steady herself. But the
next moment she was greeting him with
gentle, fluttered cordiality, thanking him
unaffectedly for remembering Pat and her
and her sister, so as to turn aside in the
course of his holiday tour of inspection to
the famous old Norman towns, in order
to pay a visit to a remote little place,
possessing hardly any interest, like
Quatr'eaux. He had never before seen
her, while entirely mistress of herself, so
gratefully responsive for a small mark of
friendly attention, and at the same time
with such a subdued manner. He liked
this new Agnes, with the shade of grief
and penitence clinging to her, and with
the transparent candour of her implied

acknowledgment of wrong-doing to himself, looking shyly out of her drooping grey-blue eyes, still better than he had been disposed to worship the old bright, fearless woman who had been so determined to do everything for herself and others, and so indomitable in doing it.

"Yes, we have lost our dear mother," she said, glancing at her mourning, while his eyes were travelling in the same direction, "and I doubt not you have heard how she lost her life in saving mine. After all her sorrows and tribulations she is at rest. Could you have believed that I should be, not only furiously incredulous as I was when you were forced to warn me that she had been betrayed into error, but utterly resentful against her for being human and fallible?" She looked up at him in wistful deprecation. "But that is all past," she added, with something of the old radiance returning to her look; "she

showed me what she was and what I was
—a poor carping, conceited Pharisee—and,
now that I am in my right mind, I am
deeply grateful to know her so much
better than I, and to seek to follow after
her last good example. We will speak
no more of this, but I thought I owed
you these few words, after I had felt and
shown myself so madly angry and out-
raged on that dreadful day when you
were only seeking to help her, and were
more merciful to her, in her extremity,
than I—her own child was."

He looked at her while she quickly
changed the conversation and proceeded
to ask after his mother and sisters. He
could see that she still wore her father's
old signet ring, while beside it, on the
same finger, was the guard of her
mother's marriage ring. And she was as
utterly free from deceit as she had ever
been. There was no more affectation
and exaggeration in her tone than had

ever existed in the enthusiastic girl who had idealized and cherished her mother so fondly. In whatever light her character might appear, either in its earlier or later development, to matter-of-fact, stolid people who had not known her intimately or come under her potent influence, her nature was clear as crystal even as it was finely tempered as steel.

Pat and Georgie were very glad to see Sam Scrope. He had not only been a friend in need, he was showing himself faithful in his friendship. He brought with him a breath of England and of their native north country, with which they were not inclined to quarrel, though they were ready to praise France—the country of their adoption—with all their hearts. The trio in the *étage* above the milliner's shop were happy and absolutely gay in the revulsion from past cares. They looked and spoke like people at ease, with nothing to make them afraid. When Sam Scrope was presented to Dr. de Vitré, and subjected, in spite of Madame Paradol's tremors, to a fire of courteous attentions from her, he behaved with imperturbable calmness. He showed himself master of his profession in parrying all her attempts to get at the bottom of such mystery as still attached to the Baldwins, who had begun by being Raimes at Quatr'eaux and had offered no explanation of their change of name.

Though madame was baffled in her investigations, she was quite ready to institute special festivities in the baffler's honour, as soon as she learnt that he was not only an *avocat* in London, but the owner of an estate in the country. What benefit was to accrue to madame from the discovery it would be hard to discover. Probably her behaviour signified merely an instinctive desire to give honour where honour was due, according to her light. Certainly she inaugurated half days in the forest, when it was glorious in its gloom under the magic of early summer, and evenings round Dr. de Vitré's microscope, when the doctor was half badgered, half coaxed into expounding the world of wonders which the little instrument had brought to light. Such attractions, though they were not much to madame's mind in themselves, did not fail even in Quatr'eaux to secure very respectable gatherings, scientific and otherwise. And in the company were included, without fail, Dr. Pierre Baldwin, the host's esteemed assistant, his sisters and their guest, with madame's consent, as well as by her brother's will. Could a distinguished stranger, M. Scrope of Scrope Hall, be at Quatr'eaux and Madame Paradol be guilty of remissness in paying him proper attention, however dubious she might be as to the history of the Baldwins whom he chose to distinguish with his friendship?

It was a sign how far Agnes was reformed from some of the infirmities of noble minds—such as pretending to herself and her neighbours that they could do something of which they were incapable, or that they were the centre of attraction in an occurrence with which they had a very minor connection—that she did not ascribe Sam Scrope's arrival to Georgie's presence. She went with her brother and sister, lionizing him and doing what they could of sight-seeing in the Cathedral and other old churches, to every quaint noticeable point in the market and the streets, and to the promenade with seats, a couple of fountains and three statues on the edge of the forest. She was one of the party in their country strolls, in the apple-blossom time when much of this quarter of green Normandy was like a great orchard.

The season recalled to Sam Scrope the
same month last year, which would
always stand out in his mind whatever
befell, whether the object of his journey
to Quatr'eaux prospered or failed, as the
May when he had first known Agnes
Baldwin. As for her, the spring got into
her blood until the springtide of her
years came back to her, so that she could
find distraction and pleasure in every
agreeable trifle in the day's record.

Since Agnes was the person in the little
family group who, if not the least engaged,
had the most command of her hours and
occupations, the duty devolved mainly on
her, somewhat to the scandal of the man-
milliner and his wife, of bearing Sam
Scrope company and rendering his stay at
Quatr'eaux as pleasant to him as possible.
She accepted her office without a demur,
doing her part docilely and naturally,
learning to talk to her companion in her
eager, sympathetic way, as she sang her

songs to him.  Pat and Georgie saw what
was coming, and were quite ready to pat
the pair on the back and say, "God
bless you, my children," for Pat and
Georgie were not the most respectful of
young people.

Monsieur and madame of the millinery
depôt laid their heads together and came
to the conclusion that *le gros* monsieur
was the *fiancé* of the pale red-haired mees
who looked like a saint sometimes, though
she was only a writer of novels.  Agnes
alone continued so little alive to what was
in the air that it was a considerable shock
to her when Sam Scrope told her, one day,
in a few words, that he had come across
the Channel to ask her whether she would
be his wife.  Her first impulse was to
recoil from the proposal.  "No, no," she
cried, covering her face with her hands
for an instant, since there was nobody by
where the pair sat, on the farthest seat
on the promenade, by the edge of the

forest. "Do you think that I could ever bear to carry *her* pitiful story into another household?"

Then he remonstrated with her in his strong direct man's way. "Agnes, if I and my suit are distasteful to you, that is one thing, and there is no more to be said. But it is quite another thing if you let a bugbear come between us and part us. For my sake, for your own, in the name of your mother, who would have held your happiness as she held your life, the first consideration, do not dismiss me because of a strained morbid scruple."

"But your mother," she said faintly, "your sisters, your neighbours in the north who knew something of the old story, had an inkling of what took place and drew their ghastly conclusions?"

"My mother," he assured her, "the moment she heard the real truth, was full of regret and remorse to think how

cruelly your mother had been misjudged.
'Poor woman! poor soul!' she cried,
'and was that all? Why, I might
have done that myself, if I had been
tempted, to save your dear father's reputation and shield our children.'"

"Ay, but it would have been out
of pure love for your father," muttered
Agnes with white lips.

He went on without answering her
words: "My sisters know nothing of the
scandal, which is rapidly dying out.
Only a very few people remember, and
they will keep their counsel; they would
be ashamed at having anything to do
with driving Mrs. Baldwin out of the
country. Besides, I should like to find
the man or woman who would make
any public statement to your disparage-
ment. As to private whispers, though
there will be little enough of them,
you could well afford to set them at
naught and live them down, Agnes; it is

the will to marry me of which there is the question, not any difficulties which stand in the way."

Yet she hesitated, and put him off with such arguments as she adopted on the spur of the moment. She had been taken by surprise, she was in mourning, it was not a time in which to think of such things. Then he had the wisdom to allow her to see that he had received letters from England which worried and depressed him. The value of land had so fallen at home that the greater part of the income he derived from Scrope Hall, subject to the usual deductions, went to furnish his mother's jointure and his sisters' portions. Mrs. Scrope had not found the neighbourhood of London beneficial to her health. The S.'s had long ago tired of Chiswick and longed to get back to the north. He had taken the resolution of giving up Scrope Hall to his mother and sisters for their home

during the term of his mother's life.
There was an additional reason for this
in the obligation which his profession laid
upon him to spend a large part of the
year in London. He did not falter in
his determination, in spite of the new
views for the future which he had allowed
himself to entertain. He continued resolute in pushing his fortune as a barrister ;
but pleading at the bar was slow work,
unless where there were stupendous talents
or overwhelming influence. He did not
pretend to either, but he was fain to think
he had some call beyond eating his terms.
At the same time he began to fear it
would be long—longer than he had rashly
hoped, before he would be able to offer
any woman he cared for a share in such
a home, as he could honestly say was
worth her acceptance. He was driven
to doubt whether he was justifiable in
seeking to pledge her to years of waiting, for he must drudge and pinch,

till he was past his prime, perhaps, before the battle was won.

She turned and fired up at once. " Who would mind working and denying themselves, Sam, if the couple were of one heart and mind ? " she declared with much of her old hope and courage. " What woman deserving of the name would not willingly, nay by preference, halve the struggles and deprivations of the man she had consented to accept for her husband ? Why, the living in shabby lodgings together, as Lord and Lady Eldon did, when they were plain Jack and Bessie Scott, of north country origin, the contriving that the little sum set aside for housekeeping money should more than meet the week's expenses, the sitting up patiently, even if she could help him in no other way, with my Lord the future Chancellor while he studied into the small hours, writing out notes of what he read for his future guidance, or

working at something else to help to fill
the family exchequer, was the very best
of the play. Don't you know it, Sam—
don't you understand it ? The excitement, the exercise of all one's highest
powers, the glad looking forward,
belong to the battle and not to the
victory. I am sure good wives always
count such years of labour and self-denial
with their husbands, as they count the
years when their children were young
around them—requiring everything at their
hands, a constant tax upon them—the
happiest in their lives. Don't tell me
we have grown so effeminate and luxurious
in our habits, or are such slaves to the
standards of our effeminate luxurious
neighbours, that couples can no longer
rough it happily together, for the love
of God and each other, like Jack and
Bessie Scott."

He took her at her word, which she
said included the condition that she was

to earn money by her calling, as he earned it by his, so that they might be joint bread-winners as well as true helpmates. He did not say her nay; on the contrary, he averred that he would not feel himself warranted in stifling and gagging her for his private ends. She would not be the Agnes he had chosen before all other women without her gifts and the full power to use them; she was quite welcome to eclipse him.

"As if I could, Sam!" she said indignantly.

The prospect of Agnes's marriage, which was to take place in the autumn vacation, brought farther changes, coming trooping, like so many ghosts, to shake the nerves and disturb the serenity of the expatriated family.

# CHAPTER IX.

## PAT AND GEORGIE'S AFFAIRS.

THERE had been a renewed proposal for all the Baldwins to return to England when Sam Scrope and Agnes wended their way thither—Pat to set up a practice where his services were wanted, Georgie to live either with him or with her sister. But Pat at once scouted the idea. He maintained that he had grown attached to France and her constitution, whoever headed the republic—he believed he could stand even Boulanger. Between him, Pat, and the girls and Sam Scrope, he believed it was France's institutions and not her constitution he was in love with. He believed that it was by a premonition that he had finished his medical studies

25—2

in Paris. He had learnt much from de
Vitré and he meant to learn more. He
was enamoured of the sciences of which
physiology and anatomy were handmaids
instead of the sciences being their handmaids. He had no great fancy for *bourgeois*
provincial society, bristling with small
etiquettes and pretensions and keen rivalries,
in which Madame Paradol loved to take
the lead. But he had the greatest respect
and regard for several of the local *savants*
with their families to whom he had been
privileged to receive introductions. He
could not say enough in praise of the
learning and sagacity of the *savants*,
which were as profound as their *ménages*
were simple, with an almost patriarchal
simplicity. To be admitted to their society
and friendship, though the occasion was
celebrated by the consumption of nothing
more substantial or costly than a cup of
coffee and a basket of cakes, or a glass of
cyder, a slice or two of Gruyère cheese

and a bowl of salad, he was willing to
barter all the swell dinners and luncheons
and all the gorgeous banquets in England.
It might be that he bartered them all
the more cheerfully because a poor "sawbones" was not likely to have sumptuous
feasts pressed upon him, and Scrope must
have attained the bench at least before
their relationship was a *carte blanche* to
rich men's tables.  He left these and other
good things to Brother Sam.  He protested
it was not because the grapes were sour,
but on account of a certain Gallic levity
which had got into his blood, that he con-
nected aldermanic turtle with vulgarity
and heaviness, and bread and cheese with
divine philosophy.  However, when his
brother-in-law was Lord Chancellor and
was entertained at the Mansion House,
Pat pledged himself to come over and
support him, even though he should be
expected to return thanks for the toast of
the distinguished strangers—he would be

as good as a stranger then, whether distinguished or undistinguished.

Georgie declared demurely that she could not desert Pat ; at the same time she did not agree with him in respect to the *bourgeois* society of Quatr'eaux. As far as her small experience went, men and women were very much the same in every climate and under every variety of condition. She had no objection to *savants*, indeed she had the deepest veneration for them, though she was not learned herself, but she thought the family of the principal *notaire*—in which there were no learned gentlemen, and for that matter no learned ladies with ill-made bodices, clumsy *bottines*, and mismanaged hair, was very nice indeed. The *notaire's* son, who was a captain in a French regiment, deserved to be called *un beau garçon*. The families of the wealthier linen manufacturers, and of the nearest proprietors, who were far above the rank of peasants,

were made up of equally agreeable people to
know, and she had enjoyed exceedingly their
birthday and twelfth-night parties, to which
Madame Paradol had taken her.    Their
*menus* were not to be spoken of in the
same breath with those at Lord Mayors'
dinners, but they were very dainty and
tasty *menus* nevertheless, and she for
one was not ashamed to own that she
asked for a little more than bread and
cheese with her philosophy.   She should
not be surprised to hear that Pat had
forgotten something in his dinner or sup-
per of herbs—a basin of excellent soup, or
trout cutlets, or a *fricassée* fowl and
mushrooms.    But that was neither here
nor there.    What was more to the purpose
was that Dr. de Vitré himself was not such
a barbarian as Pat proposed to become.
The doctor had a great deal to do, and his
favourite relaxation was sport, still he
was generally present at his sister's receptions.    He had even gone out a little

lately—to the ball at the *notaire's* and to more than one pic-nic in the forest; she had heard him say that Alix Surenne and Marie Meudon were pretty girls. He had recommended her pupils, Félice and Nicole, not to be slovens and frights though they minded their lessons, not even though they grew up strong-minded. As if *madame la chère mère* would suffer her children to be slovens or what he meant by strong-minded! That meant doctors of medicine like him and Dr. Pierre, who should in time relieve him of his practice and leave him at liberty to hunt foxes, hares and rabbits, and chase butterflies and beetles, every hour of the twenty-four.

However devoted Georgie was to Pat, and well pleased as she declared herself to be with provincial and *bourgeois* society, she was ready to tell everybody whom it might concern that she proposed to return with Agnes to England in order to see her established in her house or apartments, and be quite satisfied that her first matronly toilet was correct. Agnes was ever so much cleverer in other things, but she could not be trusted in dress and such trifles. It was not to be supposed that Sam Scrope, though he might blossom into the most erudite and astute of judges, could direct his wife—as some men were said to do in books, in her selection of frocks and disposal of furniture.

Agnes listened to the two, earnestly striving after impartiality in judging what was best for them, and in not being biassed by her natural longing to have them near her.

Then the announcement of Georgie's approaching departure in company with her sister for England for a time, produced a great storm and positive upheaval of the very foundations of the family in the *Maison de Vitré*. The storm was by no means confined to the youthful bosoms of Félicite and Nicolaise, yet they were much more disconsolate at being separated for a few months from their lively English friend, than they had been when they had stolen about on tip-toe and whispered in awe-struck voices that the English mademoiselle—the first English mademoiselle, who was so gentle and *triste*—had set herself and madame her mother on fire (their mother had said nobody could ever tell what these English, the quietest, most decorous of them, would do) and both were going to die as a result of the conflagration. It was among the elders of the household that the tempest raged most violently. Madame Paradol wept passionately where her little girls only sighed; and the deep voice of Dr. de Vitré was distinguished, raised in wrathful protest, as it had seldom been heard in his sister's company.

The sequel to the disturbance was that Madame Paradol suddenly set off with her children to a sea-bathing resort within half a day's journey. She was the soul of politeness as a rule, notwithstanding she failed to call on the demoiselles Baldwin before starting, in order to take leave of both sisters and to offer her final felicitations to the elder.

The next scene in the drama was the arrival of Pat, convulsed with silent laughter and also not without a sense of personal importance. " I never expected to be sent on such an errand," he told Agnes and Georgie in confidence the moment he entered. The former was in the pleasant flutter of looking out for Sam Scrope, who was expected to arrive that morning, after having arranged the preliminaries of the wedding. Georgie, making a virtue of necessity, was examining a small pile of articles belonging to Agnes's *trousseau*, which had just been sent up from the shop below, preparatory to their being deposited in her trunk.

" What is it, Pat ? who is sending you on an errand ? where are you going ? "

inquired Agnes, just half turning round from the window by which she was standing, and sparing him only a portion of her attention.

But Georgie sprang up from her task of spreading out gloves, unfolding ribbons and patting lace like an expert. An air of aroused interest and expectation instantly pervaded her whole little figure, while she glanced keenly at her brother, and a quiver of laughter twitched the corners of her rosy mouth.

"Behold a herald, an ambassador," cried Pat, dropping into tall language, as he also dropped on the little couch, and allowed himself, in the privacy of family life, to roll from side to side in uncontrolled merriment at the thought of the absurdity of the tidings which he was about to communicate. As he did so it was wonderful to see how his troubles had rolled off him, for he was singularly like the lad with whom Georgie had dis-

cussed Agnes as the trial of her family
in the drawing-room at Barnes. Along
with the boyishness which had re-appeared
the little fellow was not without a certain
pompous air belonging to the trusted
emissary of a greater person than himself,
the conscious bearer of news of startling
import.

" Listen, you two girls, you never heard
anything like it. I am commissioned to
convey an offer of marriage to my own
sister, Georgie there (you little wretch,
you have a great deal to answer for !),
from my chief, my boss, Dr. Hubert de
Vitré. I know I am entirely out of order
in being here on such a mission. I am the
person who ought to receive and consider
the solemn proposal on my sister's account,
and as Georgie s nearest male relation treat
with the suitor for her hand. I should not
be the man to make the offer, for such an
anomaly constitutes me both proposer and
receiver of the proposal. But what will

you have ? Dr. de Vitré can never conduct the common affairs of life like anybody else. He is as bad as Agnes, whom he ought to have married to make the mess complete. I have heard madame his sister complain of his unpracticality a thousand times. Besides, necessity has no law. He has heard that the object of his aspirations is to start for England the day after to-morrow, and he cannot let her go without a declaration of his wishes. Therefore, as madame is *hors-de-combat*, for they have had a tremendous row, because he rose up like a man—I did not think he had the courage—and asserted his rights so successfully that she was beaten off the field, and retired sulkily with her chicks to the sea-side, I tell you there is nobody left to employ on an emergency except me. So behold I am here commissioned to solicit the honour of my sister's hand in marriage for another— naturally for Dr. de Vitré."

" How stupid and unpleasant," exclaimed Agnes hastily. " I did not think
that Dr. de Vitré could be such an old
fool, a middle-aged, clever man like him—
one might have expected something very
different, though he is odd. How silly
and impertinent of Madame Paradol to go
away, without seeking an explanation. Of
course she might have known that Georgie
would have nothing to say to her brother.
It is laughable, and yet it is disagreeable
for everybody, especially for you, Pat. I
almost wonder you can laugh at it."

"I don't see anything so laughable or
absurd in the step Dr. de Vitré has taken,"
said Georgie with the greatest composure
and considerable dignity. "He is an excellent man, you will allow so much.
More than that, he is an eminent man,
better known and more esteemed in his
profession, at this moment, than Sam
Scrope is in his. I happen to know Dr.
de Vitré's age—he is a year younger than

his sister. He is thirty-nine and I am nearly twenty-three ; he is not much more than sixteen years my senior—not quite a Methuselah, you will allow," looking reproachfully at Agnes, "only the age to inspire proper respect and deference in a wife. As for his person, I think it fine, what with his height and his dark eyes. I admit he is not always dressed professionally or well, but he is always distinguished-looking. He can keep me and provide for me with perfect ease, which is more than Sam Scrope can pretend to do for you, Agnes, at present, though in addition to hampering himself with a wife, monsieur my doctor has to play the principal part in maintaining his sister and her children. To be sure, a quiet *bourgeois* country-town *ménage*, the mistress of which will not be thoughtlessly extravagant and gay, is a much simpler, more economical affair to keep up in France than it is in England. No, I do not see

anything absurd and laughable in Dr. de
Vitré's asking me to marry him," Georgie
ended, holding up her square chin with
as great calmness and with as much
reasoning power as if she had been her
own grandmother.

Agnes stood listening to her sister, open-
eyed and open-mouthed as Georgie herself
used to stand when anything happened
to astonish her. Agnes actually forgot
that Sam Scrope might be turning into
the street at that moment. Pat, who was
more behind the scenes, was taking stock
of the situation, and enjoying it without
reservations.

"You do not mean to say, Georgie
——" began Agnes.

"I do mean to say, Agnes." Georgie
turned the tables, her whole face again
dimpling over with fun.

"Georgie thinks you think there ought
to be only one marriage in the family, and
that yours," said Pat mischievously.

"Georgie thinks nothing of the kind, and I have heard of Sam all my life," Agnes defended herself.

"Yes, and it is not so very long ago since you were bent on handing him over to me, whether he and I would or not," retorted Georgie scornfully.

"I did not understand either myself or other people," granted Agnes, humbly enough. "I had got a fixed idea into my head, a kind of infatuation caused by the degree to which I was engrossed with my work, and by a conceited persuasion that I knew better than anybody what was best for you all and should dispose of you accordingly. I know better now ; I have not been so capable of meeting the claims on myself, and of discharging my obligations, that I should dictate their parts to other people."

"Nonsense," said Georgie briskly. "You have been the best of sisters, as mother always held you had been the best of daughters."

"And as Sam Scrope, poor credulous mortal, is persuaded you will make the best of wives," put in Pat hastily, as an antidote to the sorrowful recollections which made Agnes shake her head mournfully.

"I hope I also shall make a good wife," Georgie took up his cue.

"A good wife? I do not doubt that," cried Agnes, clasping her hands, "but will you be a happy one? Oh, Georgie, I am afraid you have been carried away by the French theory of marriage—marriages of esteem, of friendship, and all that kind of thing. It is very plausible what is said of suitability—though I confess I do not see the suitability in this case—and advisability, and you are quite the girl to lay such rational arguments to heart. But, oh! I can guess that a loveless marriage is an awful and evil mistake, even when both husband and wife are still resolute to do their duty. Its consequences may be as fatal and far-reaching as those of the

most selfishly imprudent love marriage."
Agnes bit her white lips in seeking to
control herself, as she recalled their mother's
loveless, hapless marriage.

# CHAPTER X.

But Georgie only cried, "You are too provoking!" speaking with the greatest animation and blushing scarlet. "I declare you think nobody is lovable but that great lumbering lawyer of yours."

"Colossuses, or ought I to say Colossi, are gone considerably out of fashion," said Pat complacently.

Georgie faced round on "little Baldwin." "Pat, will you have the goodness to remember that Dr. de Vitré is six feet two? I don't mean by that assertion," she continued in a relenting tone, "to question the north country saying that 'good gear is made up in little bundles,' or to deny the fact that many of the greatest men in the world have not been giants in stature."

" Pigmies, rather—but you had better not," remarked Pat gloomily.

" Do you, Agnes," Georgie returned to her sister, " wish me to proclaim that I adore Dr. de Vitré, with Pat there grinning till I'm out of countenance ? "

" Oh, don't mind me," said Pat modestly. " You are aware I am not here in my own character. I am simply the friend of my principal, presenting my credentials, laying before you his proposals, of which, by the way, you will not suffer me to give you the details—how he spurns the national habit of requiring a *dot* with the future Madame de Vitré—what settlements he is willing to make on her."

" Oh ! never mind them," cried Georgie ; " we can take them on trust," an inconsistent speech on the part of so practical a young woman, which perhaps as much as anything staggered Agnes in her preconceived opinion of the state of Georgie's feelings.

"I want to say how good I mean to be to this unfortunate man whom I am not supposed to be able to love. He is to get his fill of hunting in the season; so you may look out, Pat, for you will have to do double work on these occasions. He is to have the most expensive of books and instruments in prosecuting his interesting, invaluable investigations; you cannot think how stingy and grasping Madame Paradol can be in insinuating to him that he cannot afford this or that help to his studies, that it is selfish of him—of him, the most generous man, who says the least in the world about his generosity—to indulge himself in such things, when a little self-denial on her part would make the matter perfectly simple. His assistant in his experiments is never to be out of the way, or engaged, or weary. He is not to be bored with company he does not care for. He is to have the strongest *café noir*, the spiciest cake, the exact kind of soup and *entrée* he fancies. He is to retire to his room, and reappear in the *salon* just when he likes. The carriage and horses are to be kept for his use more than for any other person's. When he goes into the forest, it is that he may stroll and rest at will, and search for plants and insects, without being forced to return at set hours, or without having guests to attend to all the time. The master of the house is to have a good time of it, when the house has a new mistress. He is to be the first person instead of the last to be thought of in the establishment—which is the fruit of his honourable exertions." Georgie's eyes were sparkling and her breast heaving. It was hardly possible to remain any longer sceptical as to the nature of the emotions which inspired her

"Bravo, Georgie!" Pat applauded. "The boss will be a spoilt man and ruined philosopher in the course of three months; nevertheless, I hope my wife—

when I am in possession of that ticklish
commodity—will go and do likewise. I
hope Sam Scrope's wife will not be so
carried away by the passions of her
heroes and heroines and the *dénouements*
of their fortunes, as to forget to order his
hot joint, or to neglect to supply him
with artichokes. I trust you have noticed, Agnes, that the judicial Sam has a
weakness for artichokes?"

"But, Georgie—" Agnes resumed the
attack more hesitatingly and less directly
this time—"have you forgotten Madame
Paradol, who is apparently so opposed
to her brother's marriage? Are you
going to marry any man in the teeth
of his family's violent objection to the
marriage?"

"His family consists for the most part
of his sister and his nieces, of whom he
is the chief support. It is not as if there
were a father and mother in the case, with
the French notion that even a mature

man should submit and defer to his parents in the most important act of his life ; though if it had been so, I do not know that I should have given him up," said Georgie determinedly.

"But even with regard to madame, your openly defying her strikes me as a very un-French proceeding," persisted Agnes. "I am afraid she will be able to work a great deal of mischief—to spoil your peace, if you are to continue in the same household. I shall dread her rendering you miserable."

"She will do nothing of the kind," said Georgie with triumphant conviction. "I am not going to marry madame, I am going to marry her brother. I own I wish she had been less disagreeable at this moment ; however, one cannot get everything, especially when one is nothing out of the common. I am not a beauty or an heiress, I am not an author, I am not an artist, as you must

see by this time. Every man has not
his female relatives at his beck and call
like Sam Scrope. I know Mrs. Scrope
and the girls have each written to you—
at his instigation you cannot doubt, civilly,
nay, kindly ; and whatever reluctance they
had to write, or whatever disappointment
they experienced at the cause of the
correspondence, for mothers and sisters
are apt foolishly to hang back and be
rueful when only sons and brothers
marry, I am sure the regrets will soon
be lost sight of at Scrope Hall. They
will be swallowed down for Sam's sake
and yours, and perhaps a little for mine,
since we were all friends. Mrs. Scrope is
a kind woman and the S.'s are good-
natured girls. You will soon be a first
favourite with them ; they will be proud
of your writing, too. Real live authors—
not to say successful authors—though
they are getting dreadfully common, are
still a little rarer in their set than they

were in yours at Barnes. But I am not
an author or an artist, as I said; I am
nothing out of the common. I have no
right to count on people's immediately
throwing down their arms or prejudices
before my claims."

Pat had been silent for some time; he
had not even laughed at Georgie's allu-
sion to only sons and brothers. He was
graver than he had looked at any moment
during the discussion. "Perhaps I ought
to tell you, girls," he said with some
hesitation, "that there really was a tremendous row between Madame Paradol
and her brother about this business before
she left. They were in the *salon* with
the windows open, and I was in the
court fastening up Lion, after I had taken
him out for a walk. He was troublesome
in his high spirits, and would not suffer
me to fasten the chain to his collar without
some difficulty, while I could not let him
go, because he is sensitive as to the poor

patients, whose hour it was, and does not always distinguish them from *rauriens*, to Dr. de Vitré's annoyance. I need not say I did what I could to make my vicinity as audible to the lady and gentleman within, as their conversation was to me. I coughed and hummed a tune, I even tried to make the dog growl or bark, in vain. The speakers were far too much engaged to notice me, and strive as I might I could not help hearing a part of what they said ; my ears in spite of me seemed to grow preternaturally sharp in the fix. I could not shut them to his emphatic statement that he was old enough to judge for himself, and knew the woman who could make him happy when he had the good luck to meet her at last."

"My dear Pat, there was no occasion for your hearing that against your will, and then repeating it as if you ought to be ashamed of yourself," said Georgie

cheerfully. " But there is one good thing,
you have given me a warning. I have
always liked the court immensely. You
cannot imagine how I used to break the
ninth commandment in connection with
the Doctor's court, when the gates were
open and I ventured to peep in at
its gum-cistus bushes as white as snow
of a morning, though the snow had
all fled by night, and at the sunflowers which went on in full force
without so much as winking their
great eyes, first when we came to
Quatr'eaux and you had just been engaged as an assistant to Dr. de Vitré.
Now there are magnolias with their mag-
nificent buds bursting into blossom
where there were dainty rosebuds in May.
I am as fond of the court as ever, and
it is going to be mine—mine and my
husband's—but I must not forget when
we quarrel with the windows open, what
capabilities it has for an audience of more

than Lion and the blackbirds and night-
ingales. As for what *you* were condemned
to hear, we can guess it perfectly."

"But there was more than what I
have told you, Georgie," said her brother,
shaking his head and looking at her a
little sadly. "It was true also, but none
of us would care to guess it. Madame
told her brother that he was not only
degrading himself by proposing to marry
an Englishwoman, a girl without a *sou*,
whose brother had been glad to become
his assistant at a paltry salary, while the
girl herself had been only too thankful to
be governess to madame's children for a
still more miserable sum. What was far
worse she belonged to a family who by
their own showing, from their passing
under a false name, were under a dis-
graceful cloud when they sought refuge
at Quatr'eaux."

"Oh! did she say that?" exclaimed
both the poor girls, hanging their heads.

Georgie's glee and pride in her conquest were summarily extinguished. Agnes was wounded to the quick.

"Yes," said Pat with more spirit, "and he told her—I never heard him in such a passion; I could not have believed him capable of it—that if she said such a thing again, he must ask her to leave his house and never to return to it."

"He does not know," said Georgie faintly; "I know he ought to be—told, and," she added more firmly, raising her head and looking at her brother with truthful eyes, "some day, before he marries me, he shall be."

"There will be no need; he does know," said Pat quietly. "When I saw what might happen, I thought it was only fair to speak out, however hard it might be to say a word on the subject, to make him acquainted with the facts, in a confidential moment. I argued with my-self that the poor mother would have preferred it so, rather than that there should be any farther misleading and deception, or that the innocent should be blamed."

Agnes quivered in every nerve. It was she who had urged Pat, long before, not to suffer Dr. de Vitré to engage him under an assumed name without taking the doctor so far into his confidence, though it were at the imminent risk of the gentleman's having nothing farther to say to his would-be assistant. But she had not, up to this moment, laid it to heart that there could be anything between Dr. de Vitré and Georgie. Therefore it sounded dreadful for Pat or any person concerned to speak of their dead mother's sin and sorrow to a stranger. As if Dr. de Vitré were a stranger in Georgie's eyes! They had recovered all their courage and confidence, while she leant her elbows on the table and her face on her hands, in order to see and hear better, and cried eagerly, "Yes, yes, Pat, what did he say?"

"He did not say much," said Pat, a little huskily, "but I do not think he could have said anything more to the purpose. He pulled his moustache slowly and muttered softly, 'Poor mother! poor children!' Then he looked me full in the face, and threw out his hand, flinging away the remnant of his cigar. 'Allons, my young comrade, what is that to us?' he protested. 'We have nothing to do with it, unless it read us the lesson that the fortunate should, for that very reason, be the more tender to the unfortunate.'"

"That was like him," cried Georgie proudly, clasping her hands; "my brave Doctor—my good honest man."

When they were all calmed down again, Agnes, struggling still with an elder sister's responsibility, tried to remind Georgie that Madame Paradol, having been left early a widow, had been her brother's companion for a number of years. She had had his ear for all that length of time. She knew his ways. It was not possible that a single rupture, however violent, should destroy the associations and habits of years ; and there was she, bitterly hostile to Georgie, with a power-ful weapon to use against her.

"Say no more, Agnes," Georgie forbade her impatiently. "Do you think I would not trust *him* though a legion of such sisters were drawn up in armed array against me ? As to knowing his ways, I have learnt more of them in the course of eighteen months, than madame has mastered during their respective lives— not that she does not care for him in her way, only she cares for herself a great deal more. She has the utmost respect for the family—the de Vitré family—and when I am one of them she will not permit any one else to assail me. She

will uphold my smallest virtue in the
eyes of the public, till she will begin to
see it herself. She is not a fool. She is
a very clever woman, in another way from
that of her brother. When she finds
that the marriage will go on, whatever
she says and does, she will make up her
mind to it, as to other arrangements
which are not entirely to her wishes."

"I hope she will, Georgie, since you
will put yourself in her power," said
Agnes, still speaking dolefully.

"I shall be in nobody's power except
my Doctor's, and you do not dare to
doubt him? Besides, madame is not an
ill-conditioned person, as you have had an
opportunity of judging. She can be a
very agreeable companion, and she will
be all the more so, when she consents to
occupy her proper place in her brother's
house. She is not a demon, such as
one encounters in novels. She is well-
principled and upright, according to her

standard. I only hope I am as conscien-
tious according to mine. She would no
more conspire to murder my character or
myself, than I would plot to kill any part
of her."

"Is she not all the more dangerous
for this reason?" Agnes ventured to
suggest. "A righteous woman, beyond
suspicion, may be the hardest, most vin-
dictive of any."

"She has one very soft spot in her," declared Georgie. "She is fond, really fond
as well as proud of her children. When
she discovers that they are as dear to
their uncle as ever, and that their new
aunt does not fail to love her little nieces,
as madame knows their old governess
loved her pupils, Félice and Nicole will
be a strong bond between their mother
and the English '*ingrate*' and '*traitresse*,'
as she may be calling me, in private, for
a week or two. She is not the woman
to bear malice where malice is useless, or

to decline overtures of peace, when they
will serve her nearest and dearest as well
as herself. I mean soon to be on very
good terms with madame my sister-in-
law. I mean more than that," cried
Georgie with a dash of Agnes's old radiant
faith and hope. " I mean to vanquish her
by sheer good-will, to constrain her to be
honestly my friend, no less than my re-
lative by marriage."

" You ought to succeed," said Agnes
admiringly ; " but there is another obstacle
—there is the difference of creed."

" Oh, Agnes, you are not such a bigot
as to make that an insuperable objection," remonstrated Georgie. " Of course
I am sorry we are not of the same
mind on that as on other things ; still,
surely it is infinitely better that he
should be a good Catholic, than that he
should be an Agnostic, or an absolute
unbeliever, like many men of science."
Georgie did not wait to let Agnes

object that it was not incumbent on her
sister to select for her husband a man of
science, who must be either a good
Catholic or an unbeliever. She went on
to say : " He is as liberal and tolerant as
he is reverent and devout ; he will allow
me perfect freedom in the practice of my
Protestantism—Pat is empowered to say
that—I am sure he is."

Pat nodded.

" And only think of the help and comfort I shall be to Pat, as Dr. de Vitré's
wife," Georgie ran on exultingly. " I
wonder you, who have been so concerned
about his welfare and mine, since we were
children, do not take that into account."

" I beg you will not sacrifice yourself
for me, Georgie," said Pat, holding up his
hands in deprecation. " I could not accept
such self-renunciation ; and pray be careful
how you commit yourself and me. I trem-
ble lest you should mention the words
'partnership' and a 'double union,' a future

alliance between your humble servant and
Mademoiselle Félicité, who granted me
charily—I feel bound as a gentleman and
man of honour to say charily—a kiss, as
payment for a box of bon-bons which I
contrived to present to her and the other
pigeon, before they started yesterday.
Madame their mother called them away
very sharply, though I assert I was as
innocent as a child, myself, of either Dr.
de Vitré's or my sister Georgie's flirta-
tions. After all, madame is entitled to a
voice in her little daughters' present kisses
and future alliances."

"We shall see," said Georgie airily;
"you will just be the proper age to marry
by the time Félice is grown up."

"If we could see," said Agnes, "what
is in store for us, whether of joy or
sorrow !" She spoke so wistfully as to
subdue their chattering and chaffing. "If
you do care for Dr. de Vitré, as I believe
now you do, it is all right, and no doubt,

without joking, your marriage will be a priceless boon to Pat. I think mother would have liked this end. Perhaps *she* sees, and it was what was wanting for her to be comforted and at peace. Ah, there is Sam ; he has a great liking for Dr. de Vitré. He will be pleased. We shall spend all our holidays at Quatr'eaux."

THE END.

PRINTED BY
KELLY AND CO., MIDDLE MILL, KINGSTON-ON-THAMES;
AND GATE STREET, LINCOLN'S INN FIELDS, W.C.